Adeline Dutton Train Whitney

Ascutney Street

A Neighborhood Story

Adeline Dutton Train Whitney

Ascutney Street
A Neighborhood Story

ISBN/EAN: 9783337372316

Printed in Europe, USA, Canada, Australia, Japan

Cover: Foto ©Andreas Hilbeck / pixelio.de

More available books at **www.hansebooks.com**

A NEIGHBORHOOD STORY

BY

Mrs. A. D. T. WHITNEY

BOSTON AND NEW YORK
HOUGHTON, MIFFLIN AND COMPANY
The Riverside Press, Cambridge

ASCUTNEY STREET.

CHAPTER I.

Ascutney Street is a shady little thoroughfare, running westerly between Midland Avenue, where the horse-cars from the neighboring city pass, to Katahdin Street, which crosses it at the top.· It is in a comfortable suburb where a new district has been built up on a boom and christened with a pretty name, — Wellswood; it is pleasant and quiet, with houses of moderate air and pretension occupying the not very large lots on either side.

These houses, however, have certain modern touches about them, which link them, as it were generically, with the prouder mansions which do not stand on streets, but have private approaches from the common highway, and occupy the aristocratic seclusion of their own wide grounds. It is the way with houses and people, in these days; some touch of art, as truly as of nature, makes the whole world kin.

These little houses in Ascutney Street had, some

of them, their Dutch doors with glazed upper halves; some of them their projecting upper story and hooded windows; all had at least some eccentricity of color or contrasting of clapboard work and shingles. So Ascutney Street took rank, as it had been laid out to do, with pronounced gentility, albeit in a small way.

The people of Wellswood had conceived the idea of making the mountains sponsors for their avenues and byways; and the brisk demand for lots laid out on Ascutney Street vindicated their sagacity.

Ascutney Street was "as good as Katahdin Street," and Katahdin Street was "as good as Shasta Street," way out on the new western limit. So of course the syllogistic deduction was, that Ascutney Street was as good as Shasta Street, which is to say as good as anything on the planet need to be.

The horse-car conductors and the little boys called it "'Scutney Street;" but some travelers call the great Vermont peak so, which does not belittle it at all; and the dwellers on the happy line gave it its three distinct syllables with religious fidelity.

There were two or three persons on Ascutney Street who knew people on Katahdin Street. These accordingly ruled on Ascutney, and led the little variations and advances of style in cards and invitations, dishes and garnitures. In Katahdin Street, again, a few favored ones had friends over on Shasta; and ruled, in turn, their middle province. On Shasta, Heaven knew who ruled, or whence; as Ascutney emulated Katahdin, and Katahdin Shasta, it was an unspoken creed, I think, at the remoter end of the social order, that those high and ineffable existences did simply " emulate the angel choir, and only live to love and praise."

And why not emulate up and up, until one reaches the angels? The principle is good, — is Bible doctrine and inspiration; but possibly the grandest principle may, in practical and partial application, get turned inside out. Perhaps what they did on Ascutney Street was to mistake the outside for the in. Or, the links all there, and the line of progression plain, perhaps there befell an inevitable catastrophe of too conscious evolution; the tadpoles being in a hurry, and pulling off their own tails before they had done with them.

Only one or two ladies on Ascutney Street had two servants; only three or four more "kept a girl" at all. The rest did their own housework, with help hired in, and with a reticent dignity, nobly superior to any circumstance involved, except the carefully guarded contingency of being caught at it. The devices for escaping this were individual and original, — I may add transparent; if they had not been, there would not have been so many separate inventions diligently sought out. Each one knew perfectly well her neighbors' ways, in certain things; each, nevertheless, fondly imagined that her own brighter contrivance was her own secret. To do them justice, the credit of the whole street was so much at every heart that they would not have found each other out, — out loud, — if they could.

Mrs. Hilum had it all to herself, the getting up before sunrise, and washing the insides of her parlor windows before the break of day. Mrs. Inching had a costume, in which her own baby would not have cried for her, under whose disguise she boldly went forth of a Saturday forenoon and not only washed the outsides of hers, but cleaned off the piazza floor afterward with broom and scrubbing pail. And Miss Rebecca Rickstack, who lived all alone in serenest neatness and comfort in the little brown and primrose cottage on the corner of Thorn Lane, and whom the good managing sense of the ambitious community would hardly have justified if she *had* kept a girl, — even Miss Rickstack made her one little dodge by choosing moonless evenings to shake her rugs and doormats out on her back grass-plot, instead of otherwise breaking into an extra hour of counted service reckoned at the quarter cent a minute. Nobody ever saw the rugs shaken; the inference was plain; but if Ascutney

Street folks drew inferences, they drew them for the most part silently, and stopped short of references.

Half a dozen housewives economized by sending out the real chorewoman to perform these obvious labors, while in the inner sanctity they ironed the clothes which the hireling had washed the day before, and hung out in the sight of the neighborhood. To put the proper Ascutney Street face upon things was the one thing required by public opinion; the only unpardonable sin would have been to compromise the common self-respect by departing openly from the prescribed lines. If there were not a cook and waitress in every house, matters had merely to go on as if there were, without confession or exposure, and the status was maintained.

Ascutney Street was embarrassed in two points by this tacit observance: one fertile subject of conversation was limited, and the "answering" of bells became a problem.

Always to go to one's own door was too patent; it was also very often inconvenient, or even impracticable. Two elegant customs were adopted in general avoidance of this dilemma.

Ascutney Street folks had "afternoons." They divided a fortnight amongst them, and each lady received once in the two weeks. And for between times,— somebody had found out that on Katahdin

Street, where there was much social running across lawns and impromptu dropping in, a ribbon was tied around a doorbell in sign of absence or inevitable engagement. So it soon came to pass that here, through the busy hours of every day, there was a delicate fluttering, as of poised butterflies, of violet, crimson, blue, and yellow knots, in varying shades, all along from porch to porch; and when these were withdrawn, the hostesses were apt to be seated in their front windows, with their afghan-work or their more delicate sewing, or even with some new book that was being so talked and printed and preached about that it was equivalent to not understanding the American language not to have read it, — and thus they were prepared to meet, at the entrance, with cordial alacrity, any visitor who might approach.

The beauty of this system of signals was not only its refinement, but its sincerity; they told no lies, yet they offended no one; they were daintily polite.

Ascutney Street certainly gained by its two embarrassments; it reached at least two points of a true high-breeding: it dropped the servant-topic out of its talk, and it took up a graceful social veracity.

There is no endeavor at ascent, at whatever low incline of angle, that does not lift a little in the perpendicular. Ascutney Street had learned a primer lesson; it invaded no one's business, so far as private and unseen domestic arrangements were concerned; when it came to obvious facts and outward conformities to a severe local standard, it discussed these with the cruelties of self-defense that can risk no mistake of mercy.

Yet even these severities were a training; perhaps we can see how the world at large has come up, through some such stages, to the perception and claim of a more interior elevation; to the sense that at least there should be no "bad form" of habit or intercourse incongruous with the high character-tone to which "noblesse oblige." The forces of the kingdom of heaven bend even our earthliness toward itself.

The mere adoption of that word "form" shows much. It is an acknowledgment that act and conversation are but exponents of the hidden and only essential reality.

But I have a scrap of story to tell, and it is time I had fairly begun it.

Jane Gregory had a scrap of a story; a very scrap; the most inconsequent trifle. And yet it was a first page, — hardly that, even, — a broken sentence, — of something that might — with some other girl, — in a book, for instance, — have had a captivating middle and a lovely end. Jane sat and conned it over, — this little "to be continued;" — in

an innocent way, half-conscious that she di   .
quiet, lonely intervals that came to her often, over
her monotonous work or in her even more monotonous resting times.

Jane Gregory was a seamstress. She went out
at a dollar and a quarter a day. She felt she must
insist on that quarter, for her room, with the partial
or occasional board required, cost her four and a
half a week. Out of the rest had to come her
clothes, her car-fares, and her coal and kerosene.

Jane Gregory was as pretty as it is at all judicious
or even comfortable for a poor, unsheltered little
seamstress to be. She knew that beauty was a
snare; she had experienced that it was sometimes
an embarrassment; she knew also that beauty was
as grass, — that it could not last long, especially
with a hard-worked, hurried little sewing-woman,
always anxious about darts, and arms' eyes, and
drapes. Yet it was a great comfort to her just to
be pretty; to have that much of the joy and glory
of a living thing; to possess, in her very own self,
that much of the inheritance of the earth, of which
else she had so very little. And as to the grass-
iness and fadiness, — well, she remembered the
verse about " so clothing the grass of the field," and
thought, in her simple sort of interpretation, that
if God did that, He would so much more · do the
better other; He would so much more, somehow,

clothe that real, waiting, wanting life of hers. The grass withered, the flower faded; but the " word," — what was that but the intent and promise under the making of the grass and flower? — *that* should be kept forever. She did not exactly preach it out, but the texts came to her; she caught a glimpse through them, and she kept on with her cheerful, small, vague expectancy.

And she treasured up her one morsel of adventure; a thing that had happened to her one day, that brought to her a momentary share in something she had seen making the daily life and commonplace of girls more fortunate. It was a deferent little service, rendered to her with a pleasure of rendering evidenced even through the restraint of well-bred strangerhood; a restraint that was of itself the finer compliment.

The occasion was a troublesome little accident; but it had put her, for the brief while, in the dignity and privilege of her womanhood. She had been gently cared for by a gentle man. I like to separate those two words; they are so commonly run together, to the annihilation of their meaning.

It was on the train; she was going from Wing Street station down to Briarwood, for a day's work. There were a good many persons getting on; some slow, old people, and some women with children; besides those individuals who are on every train,

who do not know which car they wish to get into,
and who block the platforms. Jane let them all
have way, and came up the last; she was scarcely
inside the door when the train started. At the
same moment, some one just before her stepped
backward again and crowded her. She held by the
rail, and the brakeman shouted a warning; the un-
decided passenger went forward, and the danger
was over; but a sudden whirl of wind — it was a
gusty day — seized Jane's hat, and carried it back,
past the line of moving carriages, quite out of sight
and beyond rescue. They were gaining headway,
and there was nothing to be done; even the brakeman had not seen, for he had already turned his
back, holding his own hat on, to close the door of
the opposite car. Another person, however, seated
just inside that opposite door, had noted the mis-
hap, and the swift consternation that flashed over
the sweet, unshielded face.

Jane Gregory slipped into the first seat, — the
one in the corner, behind everybody. She untied
a little scarf from her throat and put it over her
head, knotting it under her chin. The young man
opposite soliloquized silently.

"Some women would have jumped off, — or tried
to; nine in ten would have screamed out; almost
any pretty girl like her would have shown some
mixed consciousness, of annoyance or adventure;

would have laughed, have blushed, have been excited.   She is simply troubled; and she behaves so
that not three people know."

He came to the conclusion that only two persons
knew; then he wondered what she would do; then
it occurred to him to do it himself.   While this brief
process of thought occupied his mind, he continued,
without staring, to read the charming features, the
modest attitude, absolutely quiet.   Then he drew
forth a notecase, and took from that a slip of paper;
it had an "R⁄" in the corner.   He wrote a couple
of lines rapidly, turned, and glanced down the car.
The conductor had advanced halfway, collecting
tickets.   He went to him and handed him what he
had written.

" Send this back to Wing Street from the next
station, will you?" he asked, and tendered also a
coin with the message.

The conductor read the slip and put back the
money.   " That's all right," he said.

The message on the recipe blank read: " Lady's
hat blown off train at Wing Street; send in by next
to parcel-room in town."

Still, — what would she do?   She might say nothing, but leave the train herself at the next station.
She might not have been proceeding all the way to
town.   As he reached his forward seat again, he
thought this; he gave another glance across at the

quiet head, the figure as reposeful as if nothing un-
usual suggested a restlessness, the face thoughtful
as with some uncertain consideration. They were
slowing up now; as the brakeman chanted out
" Pi-e–n'Avenoo ! " the doctor passed him and entered the next car before the movement of passengers prevented. He shielded Jane, holding herself so still there in the corner, her slightly covered
head turned away from the few approaching faces;
he stood before her, his own hat in his hand.

"I beg pardon," he said ; " but there has been a
dispatch sent back for the lost hat ; it will be at the
station in town within ten minutes of our arrival.
If you will keep your seat, — or step into the
inward baggage-room, — it will be attended to immediately."

Jane Gregory looked up at him with a quick
flush, but the least movement possible. It was only
that lifting of the head, that upraising of the eye-
lids, the showing of a relief and thankfulness in the
relaxation of little muscles that let go the expression
of anxiety.

"I thank you very much," she said simply.

"Where did the girl learn it all ? " he wondered.
The very freshness and genuineness of her intonation — every clear syllable uttered as if she meant
just that and all of it — was not like the usedness of
the favored class of women, whose self-possession was

the careless certainty of attention, whose thanks were mechanically interjectional. Yet the composure was all there; not a taint of common, underbred consciousness; she might have been a Vere de Vere. But she wore a very plain, — yes, an old, dress; and carried a very ordinary little satchel. Upon this, the doctor, as he bowed and turned to leave her, noticed the J. G. in indented letters. It gave him a curious sensation; a ridiculous feeling of proprietorship in the little bag. The letters were the beginnings of his own two names.

Jane sat still; she looked at no one, thereby assuming, with a passive dignity, that no one looked at her. If her beautiful hair had been of a darker tint, rolled up, as it was, and crowning her head with its twisted waves, it would have been hardly observable, perhaps, that she was unbonneted; but the fair shining of the soft blonde coils gave no evasion of indiscriminateness; it was uncompromising in its contrast with the bit of dark blue silk.

She would be late for her day; she would have to take off the extra quarter; there would be her added fare to town, — one of her trip coupons must be given now, instead of her way ticket; and there would be another eight cents back again to Briarwood.

Those were the things she thought of while she took it all so staidly, and made no sign. But her hat would not be lost, and it was almost a new one, and she would not even have to walk, bareheaded or nearly so, up the long train-house to the waiting-room, with the crowd.

Her thought came back with that to the kindness which had cared for her. If it had been given by an old lady, she would have felt warm, grateful. Who can blame her, if her pulse were a little quicker with her gratitude, because it was the chivalrous service to a woman from a man? It was something that she had a woman's right to, in the world; that in her world, was not apt, in just such beautiful sort, to come to her.

When, some five and twenty minutes after, waiting at the far end of the great station-house, — the car she had left already filling with an outward bound company, — she saw coming rapidly down the platform the same fine, well-carried figure, the same pleasant, handsome face looking at her as it approached with a friendly, not intrusive recognition, and perceived the somewhat clumsily pinned paper parcel which her fellow-passenger was bringing her with as easy and graceful handling as if it had been a daintily wrapped bunch of flowers, she certainly did experience a sudden tingle of exhilarant surprise.

"He is coming back with it himself! He might have given it to a brakeman, or anybody!"

She could not help being pleased,— glad; she who was only little Jane Gregory, going out to sew for the day. She had never been so attended to before. But there was no ordinary, silly, visible elation; she was as composedly modest as before; her eyes were almost pathetic as they lighted up again so softly with the touch of happiness in the courtesy that had come to her, and she said again, with that gentle, even emphasis, "I thank you, very much."

Dr. J. G. (we will be content for the present with knowing only as much of his personality as he knew of Jane's) received her thanks with a smile; he answered them with "No need; it was no trouble." Then he lifted his hat, with perhaps a half second's lingering in his parting glance at her face that it was certainly — "no trouble" — to look at, and departed.

Three steps down the platform some one, about entering the waiting train, recognized and accosted him. "How are you, Doctor?" and "How are you, Drummond?" were the words exchanged; and then one sprang upon the car, and the other continued swiftly on through the long house.

Jane Gregory adjusted her hat, and came slowly after. "Doctor!" she said over to herself; still following afar off with her eyes the figure that was gaining distance so fast and disappearing among the moving groups and streams of people near the gates, — disappearing into the great mass and other-ness of human life, a whole worldful with which she had nothing to do, after just that instant's co-incidence of the line of his path with hers. How queer living was; how much there was of some parts of it, — what mere points and breaths of others!

"Doctor!" said Jane Gregory to herself. "I wish he had just said Doctor who!" and then she laughed a quick small catch of a laugh, and blushed a tiny blush of which she was not at all conscious, and moved more rapidly herself to get down and around to the far opposite track where the next train stopping at Briarwood would be.

Jane Gregory's work went well that day; and she was so apt and cheery with it, and so nimble-fingered and sure with her fittings, and wore alto-gether such a contagious, happy content, that at night when she shyly said to her employer that she "had been so late in coming that she must not take the quarter," the lady answered, "Nonsense, child! you 've done a full day's work; *I'm* satisfied," and doubled up the dollar bill about the piece of silver, and pushed it kindly into her hand. Mrs. Scorrell was not apt to pay beyond the bargain or the due, either.

That had been two years, or even more, ago; all

that time the whirl and churning of the world's great change and mingling had gone on, in which her little shred of circumstance had vanished ; but it was Jane's scrap of story still ; it came back to her with its pleasantness of something that belonged to her, — its reminder of unlikeliness that was yet always possible, — its curious assurance that every fragment argued a remaining part somewhere, and that no bit of anything ever came into knowledge or experience that sooner or later did not bring a sequel of itself or something to which it was akin.

At the same time, these were feelings, not reasonings, with her ; they took no slightest shape of positive expectation. She was not weaving a romance about her incident; it only remained with her by the force of its kindly significance. It was the breath of an atmosphere, — it drifted to her as the airs did to the sailor across the long waters, from a beautiful world he should find more of, by and by.

CHAPTER II.

AND now she was here in Ascutney Street; staying at Mrs. Turnbull's; doing a little work for her; taking in a little from other people; resting a good deal, — which she needed more than she wanted, — it being the dull time; and she was paying three dollars a week for her board.

Mrs. Turnbull had employed her for a year or two; and made a "find" of her. Mrs. Turnbull had a way of discovering these work-nuggets; people of this sort before they had "got up in their prices;" and securing good service from them while they remained comparatively unknown, and working, as she called it, "reasonably." To work reasonably, meaning always, with a certain class of persons, by a curious inversion, accepting an irrationally small equivalent for toil.

Mrs. Turnbull did not share her advantage with her immediate neighbors, for reasons; but she did put Jane in the way of other work at discreet distances. So Jane was grateful, and always ready to come to Mrs. Turnbull on an emergency, and between times.

It had been a sudden inspiration on the lady's part, this present arrangement of making the girl an inmate. Jane had found it hard to pay four dollars and a half a week, especially in vacation times; she had no friends to visit, and of course little journeys or excursions were out of the question. She had to just weary on, in the stuffy little house in a crowded neighborhood, on a low, wet street where there was almost always a good deal of illness; and to go back in the fall, pale and unrefreshed, to her stitching and draping for women and girls brown and ruddy and shining-eyed from mountain or sea air, and good times that she could only distantly imagine.

One day she had happened to say something of this to Mrs. Turnbull; contrasting the nice tea she was taking with her, — for Mrs. Turnbull did not grudge a little extended hospitality like this when she was otherwise alone, and in good humor with her plaitings and panels, — with the poor fare she had to put up with at her lodging-house.

"You can't think what a treat such biscuits are!" she said.

Mrs. Turnbull knew that her biscuits were a treat to almost anybody. But she enjoyed being told of it, as much as if she had needed the assurance.

That night it all came into her head, while she

was undressing. "I don't see the reason why not!" she exclaimed aloud.

"Nor I," rejoined her husband, untying his cravat. "What is it?"

That was the way fresh subjects were usually started between them. Mrs. Turnbull began in the middle, like a modern novel; Mr. Turnbull took her up like a seasoned reader, sure that the recapitulation and elucidation would be immediately forthcoming; well, if, when once begun, they were not altogether too exhaustive.

"Only — I don't know what Ascutney Street folks would say!" continued the lady.

"Why should they say anything at all?" suggested the gentleman.

"I don't know — as they need; if I could only fix it so!"

"Fix it as you're fixing it now, and you'll do," said Mr. Turnbull.

"Oh pshaw!" exclaimed his wife impatiently; and then broke into full tide of explanatory statement, at the end of which Mr. Turnbull did not see much of either why or why not. If it suited his wife, however, all right.

"But you don't take it in!" cried she. "Can't you understand? It will be as good as a girl — all I want of a girl; — and she'll pay *me* three dollars a week, instead of I her; and she'll be good company, for Jane is nice and bright, and picks up as she goes along; and there won't be things broken, nor given away out at the back door; and *she'll* be sights better off!"

That was how Jane Gregory came to board with Mrs. Turnbull, and saved a dollar and a half a week, and had a nice room with a sunshiny window, and a flounced dressing-table, and pure air and good food, and was only too glad to "set an odd stitch," or "give a hand" at wiping dishes, to make up the difference.

There had only been one other condition, — a little peculiar, but not much to care for after all. "It would n't ever do," Mrs. Turnbull had said with frankness, "to have Ascutney Street folks know. We might as well give up our lease at once. It's nobody's business but yours and mine, and we must keep it to ourselves. It won't make any real difference to *you*, you see; Ascutney Street folks would n't come to see *me* if I kept a boarder; and they would n't come to see *you* if I said you were a seamstress. So you would n't get acquainted anyway. I thought I 'd better say it right out to begin with. And I don't suppose you got acquainted down in Bogley Street."

Of course Jane did n't; the reticence was on her own side, there. And here, — why, with the sweet, clean room and pretty house, the piazza and the

garden, the smell and color of the blossoming
flower-plots right under her window, and the shady
larch-tree in the garden, and the elm on the sidewalk, with the oriole's nest swinging at the tip of
the highest branch, that seemed to take her right
up into sky and air, herself, as she looked at it, and
found out by sympathy the oriole part of her own
nature, — with all these, what did she care for
" folks " ?

Does it strike you how lonely a girl must be,
before she can come not to care for folks ?

Jane Gregory was a very well brought up young
person.   That was what Mrs. Turnbull had said to
her husband when she had backed up to her real
starting-point in her conversation with that gentleman, and confided to him in detail what she had in
mind; or, in more applicable common parlance,
what she had taken into her head.

" She knows her place ; she won't put herself
forward ; she 'll keep to herself," she said.   Which
meant that the young person knew she had n't
any place, and would n't try to take it ; she could
be let alone as much as the people in the places
pleased.

In essential truth, Jane Gregory had not been
brought up at all.   She had been let grow up ; and
she had had certain care taken of her growing ; but
the *bringing,* — the tender leading, the going before

and drawing after, by nearness and by love, had not been hers.

She just remembered losing a father and a mother. She could recall very little of having an uncle, who was a coal merchant in an inland town, who took her home, gave her a place at his table, and sent her to school. She should have a good education, he said; after that she must take care of herself. He had a good many of his own to provide for. Ownness does not reach so far upon this little globe, where one would think it might almost all be kith and kin, as in the great kingdom of heaven.

Jane came to girlhood and womanhood, a well instructed, well repressed " young person; " she was not anybody's daughter or sister or intimate friend. She had been put in her no-particular place, and she had kept it. What a wonder it is that people do so meekly accept their denials, and that so few seize by force or audacity their loaf of bread!

When Jane came to the time — the " after that " — in which she was to take care of herself, she tried at first to teach; but she had headaches, schoolroom and anxious headaches, from bad air and stupidity and strict requirements; and then she took to her needle, which was quiet and perfectly under her own control, and rendered her accountable to only one person at a time, instead of to a lot of contradictory parents, or a school committee. And up the line of railroad, from Brankton to the great city, she had drifted from neighborhood to neighborhood, as people learned of her, and found her deft and "reasonable," until now she had been three years in the large town which included Wellswood.

In the mean time her uncle at Brankton had died, and left five hundred dollars in his will to Jane, which she had put away in a savings bank and out of her mind, as something not to be touched or thought of, until she should be in sickness and need, or until — any wonderful, impossible contingency should arise for which she should have to buy more gowns than she had use for now, and other things for which she had now no earthly use whatever.

"And about your own acquaintances? How will that be?" Mrs. Turnbull had inquired of her.

"You mean people coming? Oh, there may be messages and errands; but" — and Jane laughed an odd little laugh — "I have n't any acquaintances. Only 'aware-ances.' I have n't anything own in the world."

A girl right in the midst of things, making home and street and visiting dresses for other girls, and no part in anything herself! For a minute, the hardness of it came to Mrs. Turnbull's heart; but it was only an added strength to the argument for that which she had taken into her head, and it never occurred to her that she could do anything more about it. If it were all the more convenient for her that Jane should have no visitors complicating with her own, the fact had not been of her ordering. She simply availed herself of it; and Jane had come.

Now Jane, all by herself as she was, and because of being so, had a certain little thread of humor running through her quieted nature, that saved her from many a bitterness, hurt, and resentment. It was so funny, the way in which she was kept out of what she had n't the least desire to be in, — the way she was guarded from an observation she could not have supposed herself liable to, — among these Ascutney Street folks. She never sat in the parlor: Mrs. Turnbull never asked her to do so, though she often called her into her own room upstairs, and had her there by the day together, when there was dressmaking going on. She never sat on the piazza of an evening: " Mr. Turnbull's friends were apt to drop in, and it was awkward." If invited company came, of course she was behind the scenes: often importantly so; for it was upon these occasions that Mrs. Turnbull made application of the proviso that she was now and then to "give a hand." Well put, that, also; for it was free giving, and no lending, hoping for anything of special return again. It was her service that was special; the consideration for it was a generality.

It was even suggested, as she went and came upon her business errands, that the short cut across to Atchell's Corner was a better way for her to meet the cars, than to go and stand at the head of the street; there was the druggist's shop to step into and wait comfortably; and coming home, it was nearer if she just ran in at the back door, which was not locked, as the front one always was.

Jane accepted it all, and departed and arrived through the kitchen entrance; it had quite the air of a servant being kept; only, and fortunately, lest intervals should be observed too closely by any curious overlooker, the short way was so covered in by high fences and trees that there was but little likelihood of her being noticed or exactly timed.

Jane could play the piano a little; and it would have been a pleasure to her to try hymns of a Sunday, or to run through a simple old waltz when her fingers were tired of needle and scissors, and her spirits wanted some light relief. But Mrs. Turnbull begged her not to do it much; people would wonder if they went by; she herself was not musical, and never attempted the little she had learned long ago; the piano had come to her because it was done with elsewhere, and she enjoyed it, she said, for her friends, which meant " company."

There was only one thing Jane could do with her morsels of leisure, and only one place for her to do it in, out of her bedroom. The larch-tree in the back garden was nicely out of the way; and when Mrs. Turnbull found that Jane betook herself to its shelter to read, she had a big old wooden chair with a sloping foot-rest brought down from the attic, and set there in the evergreen shade for the girl to " take full comfort in." This also precluded the carrying out of any more modern piece of furniture, and it established the understanding that here Jane, with her book and her shawl, was to content herself. There was only one house whose windows commanded the larch-tree, and that was occupied by a person who, like Jane herself, had no acquaintances, scarcely " aware-ances," on Ascutney Street.

" I wonder why nobody seems to know Mrs. Sunderland," Jane had said to Mrs. Turnbull one day, over their sewing.

" Well, that 's it," replied the lady. " Nobody *does* know. She 's just Mrs. Sunderland, who took the house last spring. She 's got nobody with her but an aunt, — that 's what the children call her, though whether she 's aunt to the mother or the children, I 'm sure I can't guess, — and the children themselves. Nobody even knows whether she 's a widow or not. They might like to find out, if she had any sort of style. But she never seemed like Ascutney Street folks, and they have n't taken to her. She don't *dress*, and she don't dress her *children*, and her aunt does all the work; hangs out the clothes, right in broad daylight, and washes down the front steps, and all. And the furniture that went in was as plain as porridge; and nothing but brown shades to the windows, — not even a lambrequin. She 's pretty, too, and a good figure; if she 'd only do *something* like other folks, — if she 'd just wear a *bustle*, 't would make a difference."

" You mean people would call upon her ? " asked Jane, laughing.

" Well, yes ; if she looked more like it. But she does n't make any appearance at all."

"I suppose an appearance *is* necessary — in this world," said Jane thoughtfully. " You could n't know an angel, without. But then — it need n't be a bustling and rustling one, 1 should think."

Jane gave a slight twirl, as she spoke, to the wire dress-form before her, upon which was draped the black satin merveilleux with loops and scarfings and diagonal sweep of apron front, stiff with shining passementerie. "*Soft* clothing," she murmured, half to herself. "They that wear *soft* clothing are in kings' houses. I wonder if that may n't mean something about the real king's daughters, sometimes, as well as about people in common palaces."

" Common palaces! What a queer girl you are, Jane Gregory!" cried Mrs. Turnbull. " Yes, — that hitch *is* better. Why, I like a little rustling; just a crisp, fresh sort of sound, you know, of a nice, new thing. Anybody likes to step off with a touch of style, — especially in back breadths. Ascutney Street folks do; I won't deny it."

Undeniably, Ascutney Street folks did; they all went up the sidewalk to catch the cars, with an assertive consciousness of back breadths. Ascutney Street style was of the most obvious sort.

Jane Gregory did not say anything more about it then; but she knew very well that it was the obviousness that was the mistake. She had occasional employment on Katahdin Street, and even up on Shasta; and she could make closer comparison than Mrs. Turnbull. In a certain way, she was getting a nicer training and discrimination than that ambitious person would ever have. Girl as she was, and working girl, she had found out some things that showed her what the secret of sham was. It was not the aim at something better than one has, — the desire upward which takes for pattern that shown in the mount, whatever the mount or upper level may be; it was the contenting with the merely representative, behind which was always something in the higher place, that these others could not see, and had nothing to do with.

It occurred to Jane's observation, for instance, that when she had helped to make a dress of beautiful material and gracefully devised construction for Mrs. Talthrop, the Judge's wife, she herself never saw or heard of it again, after the last stitch was set. It passed to a use quite within Mrs. Talthrop's common, public round; it belonged to a part of her life that Ascutney Street only guessed at. But because there was this inner, removed something to which the lovely apparel was germane and fitting, its fashion must be reproduced in Ascutney Street, with an accentuation of detail, and put *en evidence* on horse-cars.

If the Gransomes, living gently and delicately always, asked in friends to a luncheon, and had it served in quiet, elegant little separate courses, this way of doing things filtered down by report and imitation — Jane herself was closely questioned, often — through successive social strata, in each of which it was a more distinct effort than in the last, until it came to be a stringency in every little household where it was an anxious, one-handed struggle, and needed days before and after for preparation and recovery. The seizing upon signs became an utter degeneration in realities. This deduction bore in upon Jane's mind as that of the principle of gravitation did upon Sir Isaac Newton's. It was the assertion of a law.

Discovering this, Jane got insight into deeper facts of similar relation also. Philanthropy and religion were done up in much the same way, she thought, in many places. It was truly high and fine to be interested in the lower classes; if they were only unmistakably low enough. Jane wondered sometimes what course all the benevolences would take, if, suddenly, the very miserably poor and openly degraded should all at once die of their poverty and despair, and be taken away to heaven, — or elsewhere, — and nobody be left for people to be kind and merciful to but other people very much like — perhaps intrusively or reproachfully like — themselves. If Jane was getting slightly cynical, it was because she was such an outside young creature; only seeing things as they showed, and hardly ever taken into the heart of anything. Yet she really had discovered a great law. It is in the inside world that we must live up into the next higher. Putting on expressions of it — even in beautiful rites of worship — does not do the thing at all.

Jane did not go to church very often; she was apt to be too tired; she was apt, also, not to get much good of it. When she did go, she puzzled

about it in very much the same way. Was it because the angels sing praises, that the hymns and
anthems were "rendered" by trained and culti-
vated choirs? Was it because before the throne
they adore always, that the prayers, in such sub-
limity of words, and with so many of them, went
up? Were they all, with their full meanings, in
all the hearts of the great crowd, under their furs
and plushes, and their tailor-made costumes? The
fuller the ceremonial, the smoother the recital, the
more she marveled. She could not worship so
fast, herself, — so easily. Had it all been thought
and felt, in that hour and a half, after which the
multitude streamed forth, fresh from their ascrip-
tions "with all the company of heaven," to make
little social salutations, even exchange of worldly
news and comment, and go home to dinner-table
talk of weekday things?

She supposed it was true with some, or the observance itself would hardly continue to be; but with
the many, was it earth entering into communion
with heaven, or was it a spiritual Ascutney Street
trying to put on what it supposed Katahdin Street
to do? Remember that in this, also, Jane Gregory
was the same little outside creature on the Sunday
that she was from Monday morning to Saturday
night. For it had not happened to her, yet, to be
taken by the hand and drawn in toward the truest

and the best by those who so knew it that their one
pure longing was to make others know. This was
due, indeed, partly to her external changes and un-
certainties, and partly to her own shy, reticent un-
willingness in her peculiar isolation, to put herself
forward or even to respond.

So Jane's Sundays, in this pleasant weather,
were mostly spent under the larch-tree. She could
just catch glimpses of the church costumes as they
shimmered by between the front shrubberies; all
the puffings standing off well behind, and vibrating
en masse to the high-heeled footsteps; the ladies
buttoning their fresh kid gloves as they passed
along, perhaps, and then sticking the glove hook
into the trim corsage, behind the bunch of flowers
or the delicate embroidered corners of the handkerchief that peeped forth like spreaded blossom-pet-
als in gay, soft colors. Husbands with their wives,
sisters together, friends joining each other, chatting
as they went along. It was what she made clothes
for, and then stepped, herself, aside from.

Acquaintances! If she could have chosen them,
and been really "acquaint!" For to know people
would have meant more to Jane than simply to
have them to nod to and speak with and call upon,
trying herself on with them, as she saw girls do,
indifferently, but with a certain invariable effu-
sion, with each other. To have anybody — any *one*

body — to know well, and to feel herself known to! Jane turned to her two books with a sigh.

One was a story, the other a little volume of texts. "Crumbs," or "Broken Bread," or some such. It was an old little book, and had been her mother's. For this she cared for it, and kept it by her, and conscientiously took its morsels as prepared quantities chosen from the great bewilderment, to her, of the whole Bible, where she hardly knew what to turn to. She was familiar, she thought, with all the history, old and new; and to go over and over it again, by long chapters, was not what Jane had learned to love, because, perhaps, the chapters did not yet divide themselves into their clear, distinct word-shinings, or carry through their transparencies the thread of a uniting living meaning. She did not care to tell them over, as mere beads. But the little texts said something straight to herself at times.

And who shall say that it was not straight to herself that, to-day, — for I am telling of a particular summer Sunday morning, — the message was sent, when she read, close upon those other thoughts, and that little lonely sigh: "Acquaint now thyself with Him, and be at peace"?

Was that possible? To know Him, — to understand Him, and be understood by Him, as friend with friend?

Another verse was linked with it; they stood in pairs: " Who dwelleth in the high and holy place, with him also that is humble and of a contrite heart, to revive the spirit of the humble, and to revive the heart of the contrite ones."

She wondered what " contrite " meant, exactly and purposely there ? Was it the wretched for sin, only ? " Contrite " was *bruised together*, she thought; that should be for sin, certainly; but *bruised*, rubbed harshly, pinched and cramped and pained, in hard places — were not hearts like that, too, apart from sin ? And the *heart*, — the very wanting and suffering and prisoned affection, — *that* was the thing promised to be revived, — to have its life given to it — by Him ! To " show pity upon all prisoners and captives " — was not this what these very words engaged to do ?

The Sunday air was sweet to her, breathed in with such thought; the story book lay unopened upon her lap ; a bird sung unseen in the high, hidden glooms of the larch-tree ; perhaps up in the sunshine, quite atop of the gloom ; and Jane listened, and the cheer was like a sudden music in herself ; whether she sang, or the bird sang, she could hardly tell.

All at once there came an odd little interruption.

CHAPTER III.

IT seemed an interruption; but Jane remembered it afterward as just the beginning of the rest of it; what the Bible word and the bird song had meant.

Between the Turnbulls' back garden and the narrow grounds of the next little house ran a fence of board palings, set close together, nailed to cross strips top and bottom. One of these, it appeared, was unnailed at the lower end; for it slid aside and a child's head and shoulders were thrust through. One hand pushed away and held up the paling, and the other gathered up the hem of a frock, while the little wearer squeezed herself through edgewise, and then stood upon her feet on the hither side, letting the board drop into its place behind her.

It was like the appearance of a fairy upon a stage scene; the small bright face and figure, the tossing curly hair, the look of power and merry mischief as she held herself still and upright an instant and glanced round her, catching sight, among other objects, of Jane.

"I 've come through the looking-glass," she said. "But *that* is n't the looking-glass!" She made a disdainful gesture over her shoulder at the fence and its closed breach. "It is the real one, — between the windows, over the console. I 've been here before, daytimes, — not Sundays. Are you the White Queen?"

"Are you Alice?" asked Jane, amused, and continuing the allusion.

"Yes, I 'm Alice. Alice Sunderland. That 's almost Alice in Wonderland, is n't it? But I 'll tell you one thing, I don't *really* get into the looking-glass; I kneel up and play pretend, and then slide round, out the window; then I 'm behind, you see, just the same. And if you go *through* a looking-glass, why, you finish it all up. There 's a good deal of mischief there in the parlor, though, without that. The big jar slipped off when I kneeled up, and the water and the roses are all over the matting. I tellifomed up to Aunty, and then I came off quick, quite away. When people are going to be in a fue, you had better not be there, — if you can't help."

Alice was evidently quoting, partly. As she ended, she walked toward Jane under the larch-tree, still holding up the hem of her frock.

"What have you there, Alice?" asked Jane, very much as if she had been the White Queen.

"Oh, they're uncle Hansel's mound beads. I borrowed 'em. They were hung over the handle of the jar. Mamma *lends* me things; things to look at, — and pencils, to write; and sometimes her stylo pen. But she does n't *give* me things, because I lose 'em, and forget to put 'em back. I'll lend you these, if you want me to." She put a great heap of strung shells — a yard or more in length, all gathered up together — into Jane's lap. They were very queer, with a dead color and a worn surface, as if they had been eaten into smoothed roughness by some long action, of water or otherwise. They made Jane think of tiny skulls.

"They came from way out West," said her little visitor. "Don't you think they're pretty?"

"Very — curious," said Jane, holding the long double festoon across her hands. "Yes, I like them very much."

"They were dug up; they'd been in the ground a long time, with heaps of other things. And *people!*" she whispered mysteriously. "Do you live here?"

"I stay here," said Jane. "And I'm very glad to see you. Only don't you think Aunty will be looking for you?"

"I don't want to go while she's looking *this* way," answered Alice. "When she's gone upstairs, I will. But I shall come again. Are n't you ever here daytimes?"

" Why, this is daytime, is n't it ? "

" Well, — it is n't *bed*time. But Sunday does n't seem a day, exactly. It 's a kind of a — long, shiny stop. There! I hear Aunty, way round by the barnhouse. We have n't got any real barning in it, — of horses, you know, — out here." And Alice darted off as suddenly as she had come, slipped through the broken paling, and was gone, leaving the string of mound shells in Jane's lap.

What was she to do with it? It must be returned, of course. It would not be safe or neighborly to hang it on the fence. The child might not come back for it until another Sunday reminded her, unless there were a search made for it. Would it be better to wait for that? It might not be noticed, or thought of, at once. Jane thought she must go round with it, and immediately, before all the people were coming down the street from church. It was a bit of a happening also, and she had not had anything happen to her for a great while. She also would go through the looking-glass.

That for her, however, was around by the street, under the shady elms and maples, — a moment's turn, which brought her to the front door of Mrs. Sunderland's house, left open by Alice in her hurried entrance while Aunty was in the rear premises. Jane stood upon the porch, just lifting her hand to the bell, when Aunty appeared through a door at the back of the hall; a somewhat slow and portly personage, evidently out of breath.

"That child!" she panted. "If it is n't one thing, it's another; and just what you can't expect or get ahead of, always!"

"I beg pardon," said a gentle, deferential voice; and then Aunty saw Jane at the door.

"I beg pardon too," she said, as she came forward. "I'm cross and flustered, and talking to myself. I can stand anything but being wee-wawed!"

What that meant, precisely, Jane did not stop to consider. "I came to bring back these"— she was beginning, when Alice's voice, from the head of the staircase, interrupted her in great excitement.

The child had a tiny bell in her hand, which she tingled, and then called out "Hullo!" She was "tellifoming."

"Come quick, Aunty! Rick's half out of the window, and he won't mind me!" and then as Aunty hurried to the stairfoot, and seizing the rail swung herself round the newel-post to the ascent, the little figure, which had disappeared in its flashing way from the top, came flying back, and another call, in two words only, hollow with dismay, smote both listeners direfully.

"*He's out!*"

Poor Aunty stumbled and fell forward, up the steps. Jane sprang past her, she hardly knew how, and rushed to the upper floor, following the little girl into a bedroom where was a low open window in the farther opposite corner.

She hastened to it, saw that it gave upon a narrow sloping hood over a small portico below. No one was visible anywhere but Alice. There was no sound, either.

If the child had fallen!

She turned trembling, but with all speed, to the staircase, and was at the foot again on her way to the spot beneath, not even noticing that Aunty had picked herself up and was doubtless preceding her in the same direction, when a shrill little pipe called out exultingly from overhead, —

"I wasn't out! I was only hided in the curtain!"

Jane sat down, strengthless, for an instant, upon the lowest stair. But she rose directly, and went to meet Aunty, coming in through the parlor from the portico. "It can't be!" the poor woman was gasping. "He isn't there! but the Good knows *where* he is!"

Jane's first words, "He's safe; he's coming," were half lost in Aunty's own ejaculations.

"I'm right here! I *was* good! I didn't

tumble!" Rick himself continued to announce, and one foot foremost, came rapidly paddling down the stairs.

Aunty sat down, in her turn, upon the nearest thing, which was the floor. Her face grew paler yet, she slipped into a heap, and lay there. Jane ran through to where she knew the dining-room must be, came back with a pitcher, placed Aunty flat, poured water into her own hand, and wet her face.

"I'm not faint," Aunty whispered resolutely. "I never fainted in my life. But — I — can — *not* — bear being — wee-wawed! Pulled — first one way — and then the other, — you know, in my work — or in my — feelings!"

"You've been the death of Aunty, Rick!" said Alice's voice, solemnly, over the balusters. "She always told you, you would."

Aunty faintly laughed, and with that the revulsion came, and she sat up, bursting into tears.

"I ain't! I ain't *not!*" shouted Rick, standing in the parlor doorway. Then suddenly he turned and ran out at the front door and down to the little gate.

"Mamma, — mamma!" they heard him begin, and go on brokenly and in a choking haste. "I ain't *not* been the death of Aunty! I did mind, — I was good, — I didn't *not* tumble out, — I just hided (a quick, eager catch of breath and a sort of spasmodic swallow at each gap between his words) from Alice, — and Alice — went — and frightened — Aunty, — and Aunty — sat down — to rest a little — on the floor, — and now — Alice — is coming down — to — zadgerate!"

But Alice was not coming down; she was standing still upon the stairs; a little confounded by all that had resulted from her imaginations this morning.

Mrs. Sunderland came in, leading little Rick.

The same sweet, quiet figure of a woman that Jane had had glimpses of, sometimes, across the garden way, or on the street. A lovely face with a tradition in it of some sort of life that Jane knew belonged elsewhere; a plain gown of soft gray summer serge, straight-hanging save for one graceful lift and loop from side to back, a round shoulder cape, a straw bonnet with white ribbon knotted with a few green leaves beside the crown; notwithstanding all the simplicity and quietness, a movement and expression bright and vigorous and self-contained enough to account for her being the mother of two little originals like Alice and Rick; such a presence was this of the unnoticed neighbor, the woman who made no appearance, and whom nobody called upon.

She went straight to Aunty, who was trying to

stop her tears, and had got upon a chair. " What was it all about ? " she asked tenderly.

" Oh, nothing, — now it 's over," was the reply. " I 'll tell you just as soon — as I get myself fairly shook together."

Mrs. Sunderland left the room, and came back presently with two small glasses of wine. She made Aunty take one, and handed one to Jane. "You look pale, too," she said.

"I beg your pardon," Jane began, as she had begun before. "I only came to bring back" — she looked round for the string of shells. "I 've dropped them somewhere ; they were some beads that the little girl brought over and forgot."

"Never mind ; sit down, please, and drink the wine."

Alice came in now, to her mother's side, bringing the beads, which she had found upon the stairs. "I *borrowed* 'em, mamma," she said, "and I went through the looking-glass, and I found — Is she the White Queen? " she whispered.

Mrs. Sunderland glanced at Jane, who was still standing, and smiled. "I should think not," she answered her little daughter, in a gentle aside. "I do not think she looks like her at all."

"No," Alice whispered again ; "the White Queen was square and chunky ; but — she might be *another* white queen, — a nicer one, you know."

Jane was tall, though I have called her little; she was only little in a social, historical sense; she had a dignity that came of much keeping of her own position; and her face was fine, as well as pretty. Mrs. Sunderland, as she looked at her, was puzzled how to place her here, in Ascutney Street.

"I found her in the garden," Alice went on aloud, "and she knew I was Alice, and she understands Wonderland; and I told her about the beads, and then I came home, and then Rick"—

"I think you will have to tell me one thing at a time, Alice," said Mrs. Sunderland. And again she begged Jane Gregory to sit down.

But Jane recollected that she must be gone. She had taken a sip of the wine, and now she set the glass upon a table. "I thank you very much," she said; "but if you will excuse me, — they will be coming home, and would you mind if I went round by the back way?"

"Not a bit, if you wish," said Mrs. Sunderland. "Only I have n't had time to understand, and I 'm sure you have been very kind. Won't you come in again, — either way?" she asked, smiling.

Jane looked into the sincere, beautiful eyes. "I would, if I might," she said. "I wonder if I may."

"I wonder very much why not?" said Mrs.

Sunderland, with some meaning. "I wonder — But I will ask you other things another time." She gave her hand, in a warm, friendly way; then Jane went, with a vague, happy sense that a new door had been opened to her, into a pleasant place, and that, for once, not with needle and scissors.

CHAPTER IV.

IT was one of Mrs. Turnbull's afternoons. Mrs. Inching and Miss Rickstack were in the parlor. It was a warm day, and the front door stood open. Street neighbors would step in without ceremony. If anybody did come from further off, Mrs. Turnbull could easily meet the visitor at the threshold. She sat within view on purpose, so there was no need of door-tending.

Jane was hemming pillow-cases, sitting under the larch-tree in the old chair. She had on the same white, thread-checked muslin she had worn on the Sunday, four days ago. Alice Sunderland, from a perch lower down in the garden on her side, where a "lovely rock" sloped up to the fencetop, and an apple-tree leaned over, discovered her; in consequence, and because of a certain promise in regard to Wonderland and the looking-glass, she hurried in and upstairs to her mother.

"Mamma, I said I'd tell you. I'm going through the looking-glass. The White Queen is on her throne. I won't borrow anything to take with me; and I won't do any mischief."

"How is it you get through the looking-glass, Alice?" asked Mrs. Sunderland.

"Oh, don't inquire things, mamma! it breaks it all to pieces!"

"Your going through?"

"No, no, mamma! your — anybody's knowing how!"

"But I ought to use my judgment about it, Alice, don't you think? How can I give you leave without?"

Alice considered, a little nonplussed.

"Mamma, why can't you lend me your judgment?" she asked gravely. "I'll be very careful of it!"

This was hardly to be resisted.

"Are you sure there's no danger? you won't get a tumble?"

"Oh, no, mamma! I *could n't* tumble! it's only just" —

"Well, you need n't tell me. And you won't tear your frock?"

"I can't — ever — be *quite* sure about my frock," said Alice slowly; "but I don't think it would, if I wrap it tight."

"Very well. Remember you've borrowed my judgment. It is a thing I am very particular about."

"I'll be very particular indeed, as particular as

if it were my own," Alice answered with most responsible probity.

Mrs. Sunderland meanwhile had been writing three lines upon a card.

"Take this to the White Queen," she said.

Two minutes afterward the loose paling was swung aside and the bright little face peeped in under the thick shadows upon Jane. A small hand held up a bit of something white. "May I come in?" said Alice.

"You appear to have a ticket," answered the White Queen. "Only the Gray Cat is the door-keeper, and the Gray Cat is also a policeman and has had to go away. He has just arrested a mouse for petty larceny."

"Oh, how delightful you are!" cried Alice, coming forward. "What is petty larceny?"

"Small thieving; borrowing without leave."

"Who told the cat?"

"Oh, the cat knew beforehand. That is what his smellers are for."

"Did n't the cat know I was coming?"

"Perhaps he smelt the ticket too, and he did n't smell anything borrowed, this time."

"No. Mamma lent me her judgment, herself; of her own decord, almost," said Alice. "And she told me to give this to you."

Jane read upon the card, "Do you not mean

to come over? Can you not give me a half hour
to-night after tea?" In the middle of the card was
engraved delicately, "Mrs. Richard Lee Sunderland."

Jane took a pencil and a small memorandum pad
from her work-basket. Upon a leaf from the latter she wrote, —

"Thank you very much. I will try to come.
JANE GREGORY."

"When you go home, you can carry that to your
mamma," she said, doubling the paper and laying
it back for the moment with the tablet. The card
she slipped into a pocket of the basket-lining.

Alice looked at her with appreciation. "I
think you are *very* polite," she said.

"Did you think a white queen would be not polite?" asked Jane. "I hope you will sit down and
stay a little while. There is quite room in this
wide chair."

"Oh, I couldn't think of getting up into your
throne!" said Alice. "May I sit here, on the
cricket part?" and as Jane moved to the right and
turned a little sidewise to keep her needle hand
free, making an open place beside her, the child
took contented possession of the vacant end of the
long foot-rest. She drew a breath of deep satisfaction. "It's so nice to have it all come real,"
she said. "It's fatiguing sometimes to pretend

everything yourself, don't you think so? But perhaps you don't pretend?"

"No, I don't. But I think it would be — very fatiguing."

"Does everything come real to grown-up people?" asked Alice. "Don't you *have* to pretend?"

"It 's a great deal better not to. Something comes real. It is better to be satisfied."

"Only while you 're waiting, between the things. Oh, I think I shall always want to pretend just a little," said Alice. "I 'm so apt to feel in a hurry. But I forgot, you 're the White Queen, and you 're in Wonderland. Everything pretends itself in Wonderland, and everything comes right off."

"Does it?" asked Jane. "There 's the cat."

"Where 's the mouse?"

"Oh, the mouse is executed," said Jane solemnly. "That 's what happens to people who take things in a hurry, that don't belong to them. You see it is best to wait."

"Well, I think the cat would have got the mouse all the same," Alice retorted. "You said he was beforehand ; and I think he 's taken a good deal that did n't belong to *him !*"

"What did it say on my ticket?" she began afresh, when there had been no immediate answer to that last.

"Something very polite — and kind."

"Mamma always is."

"I am going to see her, by and by."

"Well, she'll be glad. Only nobody must come to see *you*, right *here*, except me."

"Nobody at all?"

"Well, not anybody that does n't believe in Wonderland, at any rate."

"Will that keep out a great many?"

"Most everybody. You see they don't believe enough to really — *pretend*. I don't know about mamma, even; she likes it, — she thinks it's pretty, — to tell me; but I 'm afraid she 's got over it herself, since she used to play Hansel and Gretel with uncle Hans, — oh, that 's a pretty story!" she broke off to exclaim, clasping her hands. "Don't you think, — your majesty" — suddenly returning with those two words to the tone and manner of Wonderland, "that it 's when people are grown up and can't believe enough to really pretend, they have to pretend they believe?"

If a little bell had not tinkled out of Alice's nursery window just then, it is hard to say into what corners of difficulty she might have led the White Queen with her questions; but hearing that she sprang to her feet.

"Oh dear! give me the note," she said. "I

must go ; that 's my tea-bell. And you 'll come, —
you 'll come quick, won't you ? "

"Dear little child, I 'll try," said the White
Queen. And then Alice put up her hands about
Jane's neck and kissed her. Jane Gregory could
hardly remember when she had been kissed before.

CHAPTER V.

JANE went out in the twilight at the garden gate, through the little court which was the short cut to the druggist's corner, and so into the garden gate at Mrs. Sunderland's. She walked up the alley-path beside the fence under the apple and pear trees, and then crossed over to the side entrance in the angle of the little house. It was quite the proper door for her to come to; the degree between parlor and kitchen which it represented was precisely her own.

Mr. and Mrs. Turnbull were on their front piazza, airing their leisure and their proprietorship. Jane had washed up the tea-things; so Mrs. Turnbull had been able to keep on her company attire. Nobody thought where Jane was, so that she was not in the way; and Jane was glad there was one house in Ascutney Street not tabooed to her through being the habitation of any of the discrete order to whom her own neighborhood and its circumstance must by no possible means or accident be made known.

As sometimes happens to those who take a lower

place, Jane's choice of modest entrance led her straight to special privilege, for at right angles to the door at which she was about to ring, a window opened down to the floor, from the corner of the little back parlor. Just inside sat Mrs. Sunderland, in her low, wide basket chair, beside which a table, also low and wide, held writing materials and sewing and knitting baskets on its double *étages*.

"Don't ring; come right in here," said the pleasant voice at Jane's elbow; and the sash was pushed up higher from within, and Mrs. Sunderland stood back to let her enter.

"I'm glad you came neighborly, not as a caller," she said, pulling nearer another low wicker chair set on small rockers. "There! now you're right in my intimate corner; only it hasn't been intimate, yet, with anybody but the children. Miss Gregory, I'm going to begin on the puzzle at once. What is the matter with the neighborhood, — or with me? I've been here six months, and not a being has approached me — from less than three miles. I thought" — but here Mrs. Sunderland checked herself, and waited as if for an answer to her question.

"I don't believe I can explain," Jane said. "I don't belong here, myself. I don't quite understand" — and then she laughed. "It's atmosphere, — Ascutney Street atmosphere," she added, as if she might be thought to mean a repellence of some sort on Mrs. Sunderland's part.

" Oh, atmosphere !   Airs ? "

" Atmosphere is made up of airs, I suppose," Jane answered.   "But, Mrs. Sunderland, I don't think you know about *me*.   I am not one of Mrs. Turnbull's family."   In the second pause she made she did not notice the flit of amused expression that played over Mrs. Sunderland's face, just lifting lip and eyebrow with an " I should think not ! " of acquiescence.   " I have — an arrangement — with her, for a while ; that is all.   I am only a seamstress, Mrs. Sunderland."

" You are only the one lady I know of — as yet — in Ascutney Street, Miss Gregory," returned Mrs. Sunderland.   " The others seem to have sent me to Coventry."   And a gay laugh of utterest fun broke forth as she spoke the words.

" It 's an idiotic shame," observed Jane Gregory, making a mere statement without the slightest emphasis.

" Why, you treat it gravely ! " said Mrs. Sunderland quickly.   " Do they say any evil of me ? "

Now Mrs. Sunderland was a born diplomate, with all her absolute sincerity.   She knew which key to touch by instinct.   Perhaps it was her inheritance ; at any rate, she could not help it.   She

discerned at the outset that this girl, this seamstress, who stitched from house to house, had nothing in her of the low or small; that she would not
retail silly things that she might easily know; that
she would not secretly turn against those who had
employed her, repeating any foolishness, even if it
were such in her own estimate only, to which such
employers could have nothing correspondent. She
would not tell of them what she thought they ought
to be ashamed to have told. But Mrs. Sunderland
wanted to know; to have the full fun of it; and to
study Jane Gregory a little further in the experiment besides. So she asked, with tentative purpose, " Do they say any evil of me ? "

Jane sprang into the trap. Defending Ascutney
Street from suspicion of malice, she betrayed its
littleness.

" Oh, no, indeed! it's only, — why, it is too absurd to *be*, to say nothing of explaining, or mind-
ing. I think — it was — first — the children's
blue denim garden suits; and then — you did n't
dress — so that they could be impressed by it; and
— they have seen — your aunt — hang out the
clothes."

Mrs. Sunderland clapped her hands, and gave a
musical little shriek. " Oh, what fun ! " she cried.
" My aunt ! Do go on ! "

" Not to make fun, Mrs. Sunderland. Only to

show you how very little it all was. I think I 've
said all I ought."

" Just exactly all," was Mrs. Sunderland's reply,
in a quite different tone. " I won't ask you a
word more. I 've been making the most delicious
mistake that ever was, you see ; only you don't see,
for I can't quite explain it to you. But — my aunt!
Why, Miss Gregory, Aunty is, — I 've almost forgotten the rest of it, — Anastasia something, I believe ; but ' Anty ' ever since I can remember her
at home in my mother's service ; and ' Aunty ' to
the children from the time they could first speak.
Of course she hangs out the clothes ! she does everything ; and likes it better than when — if —
there were half a dozen more to do one thing — or
half a thing — apiece. Poor dear Aunty ! so there
came along a blackbird and nipped off *her* nose !
Mother Goose illustrated ! " and the gay, sweet
laugh chimed out again.

" I beg your pardon," seeing that Jane could do
nothing but sit silent ; " but if you could see just
what I do, — *my* going through the looking-glass !
I wanted to ask you, are your arrangements with
Mrs. Turnbull quite permanent and exclusive ?
Can nobody else have a bit of you, — for a week
or two, at least ? "

" Oh, no — yes, I mean ; I go out whenever I
can. It is the dull time now. It is only when I

am not occupied anywhere else " — There Jane
stopped, as approaching too nearly detailed explanation which she was not at liberty to make.

"I see," said Mrs. Sunderland. But she did
not see ; she only thought Mrs. Turnbull got sewing, and possibly other service, from Jane, at these
intervals, in return for her board.

"I would like you to come here, if you would.
I have needlework to put out ; but I would rather
take the needlewoman in, — if it could be you.
Shall we try each other for a fortnight? A month
would be better, if I might ask for it."

"I thank you. You are very kind." Jane answered with the same genuine, deliberate utterance
of each separate word that we have noticed before
to be her way. "I will come for the fortnight ;
and then, if it seems best, it can be the month,
— the rest of it, — afterward. Did you mean to
stay, or only by the days ? "

"And go back to Mrs. Turnbull for the nights ?
No, indeed. I want a little of your leisure, to put
with mine and the children's. Alice has taken
such a — loving — to you, Miss Gregory."

Jane did not repeat her thanks. This could not
be thanked for in words. Had she got among the
angels ? But I think Mrs. Sunderland understood her muteness.

At this moment the children came running in,

followed by Aunty.   Jane sat in the shadow, and
they passed her, going to their mother. " May
Aunty light the moon ? " they cried.

Yes, Aunty might light the moon ; the sky-moon
would not be lit to-night.   Jane sat still, waiting
to see what would come of that.   A lamp, of
course, she supposed ; these children were so imagi-
native ; nothing was in the ordinary to them.

A match snapped and flickered ; by the light of
it Jane saw Aunty lift the top hemisphere of a
great white globe that hung in the middle of the
room over a table.   The flame was touched to a
lamp within the shade, the upper half replaced,
and then was seen, hung by delicate chains to a silver equatorial line, a fair, soft, planet-like thing, in
pure white glows and dusks of carven work on ala-
baster, that shed a tender radiance through all the
room, and was itself an apparition of delight to
look at.

Jane uttered a low exclamation.

" Pretty, is n't it ?   It is the children's moon.
I brought it from — Ah, yes, Alice," she interrupted herself opportunely.   " Your White Queen
is here ; the looking-glass leads both ways."

They sat a little longer in the fairy light, Jane
talking with the children ; then they all said good-
night, for Aunty came for the little ones, and Jane
rose to go.   But it was settled, in the moment on

the porch, after the children were upstairs, that that day week should be the beginning of the fortnight.

Mrs. Turnbull came into Jane's room just after the latter had taken down the fastenings of her hair, and stood brushing it before the glass. The lady had over her arm a polonaise of peacock-blue surah, and some breadths of dove-colored silk.

"I just wanted you to look at this," she said. "I guess we can make a combination with them, and I thought we'd take hold of it to-morrow." And she went on with intricate suggestions of "letting in some side puffs, and putting on a plaiting, and finishing with an edge of lace across the front, and a heading of some iridescent bead trimming."

"I'll begin, if you wish," said Jane; "but I have a basque promised to Mrs. Storrie, and a week from to-day I am engaged for a fortnight. I will do all I can."

"Oh dear! and Mrs. Hilum's lunch is Tuesday! The Flyes are there, from New York. I wanted it to wear!"

"If it could be a little simpler, — I might try; I'll finish the basque to-morrow, and there'll be Saturday and Monday. Maybe we need not alter it so much."

"Oh, I hate *simple* things!" Mrs. Turnbull rejoined, with an indescribable nasal contempt in the utterance of the first syllable of the adjective. "And I want it to look *entirely* different from what any part of it ever did before. That's the beauty of combinations. You can transmogrify, and not show the vamping up."

Mrs. Turnbull waived the fact that she herself knew every shade of color and inch of trimming that her intimate friends had ever worn, and could trace them, with perfect accuracy and unflagging interest, through all after-adaptations; and that kindred methods made all women keen.

"But where are you going next week?" she asked curiously.

Jane threw back her flood of fawn-brown hair upon her shoulders, and leaned over the polonaise, examining something in its construction.

Mrs. Turnbull was easily diverted. "What hair you *have* got, Jane!" she cried. "Now if I could match that color in a silk! It isn't caffiolay, nor old gold, nor furlmort; but *how* it takes the light!"

Jane stood back again, and resumed her brush quietly. "I like my hair," she said, much as Mrs. Turnbull might speak of a bonnet that pleased her; and her fingers slipped along its shining length half caressingly. "Hair is such a beautiful thing."

"How funny you are! even with a compliment. But you don't *do* anything with it!"

" My hair ? I enjoy it. It is all my own."

" Of course. I can see *that*," returned the accentuative lady, " when it's all down." Jane did not explain her different meaning. " But when it's up, — it's pretty, of course ; but there's no sort of effect to it. It would look like another thing, if you'd dress it, — as I do. *My !* if *I* had such hair ! "

Jane glanced at the reflection in the glass over her shoulder — she would not have looked more directly — of the mass of bang and finger-puffs and coroneted braid, and could not resist saying, " Yes, it would be quite another thing. But I should need to be quite another person."

" Perhaps that's it. It might not be so suitable. You're a very sensible girl, Jane, if you are queer," Mrs. Turnbull answered serenely.

But she took an agitated tone again as she suddenly reverted to her former subject. " What in the world *am* I to do for Tuesday ? And where *is* it you are going on Thursday ? "

" Mrs. Sunderland wants me ; and I have promised."

It had to come.

" Well, I *must* say ! " ejaculated Mrs. Turnbull. What she must say she did not proceed to state. Perhaps it was not easy, in due order and force, to extemporize it. She gathered up her peacock and dove colored stuffs and went off to her own bed-room.

On Monday night a little twisted note came over from Mrs. Sunderland to Jane. Alice brought it; to the front door this time. Mr. Turnbull, smoking his cigar as he walked about among the little shrubberies in the front yard, took it from her at the gate. Mrs. Turnbull sat on the piazza, and said nothing. Children were such an entering wedge, she thought. Mrs. Sunderland was Jane Gregory's acquaintance; and Alice had on a plain gingham frock, and an old-fashioned white pina-fore.

This was the note: —

"Please come on Thursday at eight, precisely; I have a reason. And for a reason, or a fancy, please come up the little outside staircase from the garden, at the very back, and enter at the door you will find unfastened at the top.

Yours truly,

M. G. SUNDERLAND."

At eight o'clock on Thursday the children were at breakfast with their mother in the dining-room on the other side; Aunty was busy attending upon them; Jane crossed the garden and went up the flight of steps that ran from the grass ground to a small square landing at the very end of the building above. A door here, half glazed and screened

with white muslin, led her into a plain but exqui-
sitely dainty little room, a half-square rectangle in
shape, whose length took the whole cross dimension
of this extended portion of the house.

A white straw matting covered the floor; two
soft white sheepskin foot-rugs lay upon it, one by
the bedside and one before the tiny fireplace in the
outer wall, where stood a large, comfortable cane
chair, with cushions covered with white dimity. A
dressing-table made of a packing-box and flounced
with the like material, a white pine bedstead with
dimity spread and pillow - scarf, a white pine
washing-stand with rods above it plentifully hung
with plain towels that shone with fine ironing and
were precise in evenly creased folds, nicely fitted
fresh white window-blinds, — these were the other
furnishings. Holland shades of dark, cool green,
between the white ones and the sashes, and three
jacqueminot roses in a slender glass upon the dressing-table, were the only relievings of color. Over
by the further window a light sewing-machine
table was placed sidewise ; a white cover laid over
its working parts.

Jane stood there, making just a corresponding
bit of delicate tint and prevailing whiteness, in her
cambric dress with its tiny pink sprigs far apart on
a fair ground. She stood there still, taking in the
prettiness and sweetness all around her, when steps

were heard coming along an inward passageway : little, hurried, eager ones, and others, as light, almost as quick, but differently measured. Mrs. Sunderland was speaking to the children.

"No ; you have never been here before ; it has not been open. But now, you see the way. There is the looking-glass. You may knock three little knocks upon the door beside it."

Three little single knocks sounded ; then a very audible half whisper, — "Me, mamma, too ; let me ; " and just as Jane had her hand on the knob there came three more, rather faster and lower down. She turned the latch, drew herself back as she gently swung the door quite in against the wall, and Rick and Alice entered, curious, excited, delighted. Mrs. Sunderland stood in the doorway. Across the outer panels, now folded into the chamber, hung a large square mirror in a light frame.

"There, Alice!" said Mrs. Sunderland. "This is a nearer way. When the White Queen is here, and would like to see you, there will be the looking-glass, and you may knock. When you cannot come in, or she is not here, it will have disappeared, and the door will be fast. Thank you," she said to Jane, "for playing into my little plan. I hope you won't object to what it leads to. The children have been getting very lonely. You must not let them come upon you too much ; but when you can have them, the other matters are quite secondary, please understand."

" I thank you, Mrs. Sunderland. I do understand ; and I am pleased, very much. I am so glad to be in their little story. I 'm sure it is in me to be fond of children, though I have n't had much chance to realize it. It has been just as if they were birds ; I always long to get close to them and coax them into my hands, but I never expect they will let me catch them."

The truth was, Jane, in her outside feeling as regarded everybody, was absolutely timid with the children of those who admitted her to no sort of personal relation with themselves ; and more especially so, the more the little people were fenced off by airs and costumes. She made the fences herself ; she approached them only to do that ; afterward, they were separated from her by her own handiwork and devices. She knew it was an utterly senseless feeling ; but it got the better of her, none the less.

Mrs. Sunderland opened a deep drawer in a wall-press beside the chimney, and showed Jane a pile of nice white stuffs — flannels and cottons and cambrics and Hamburg edgings ; a basket upon a shelf above held threads and needles, buttons, tapes, and all such things.

" I have set up this place for you ; it was easy to

fall in with Alice's fancy. You have a white realm, you see; and as I wish you to take full authority here, it is well you are installed as the White Queen. There is nothing to manage children with like a little myth of their own to handle them by."

Meanwhile, Alice and Rick were reconnoitring eagerly. "Why did n't you tell us of this place before? We thought it was only a closet."

"Well, you see what the closet opens into, now the time has come. It was full," she explained to Jane, "of trunks and bundles and all sorts of unbestowed lumber, until within a week. And I discovered it would make such a nice little sewing-room."

"Mamma!" cried Alice, finding and opening the door upon the outside landing. "Why!" turning round and round in bewildered recognition; "we have played up and down these steps, and they did n't go anywhere but to the platform. Where was this door?"

Mrs. Sunderland came out and pulled across the entrance a sliding shutter that filled up with a flat board surface from floor to eave the space between the upright beams that served as doorposts. "That shuts it in, safe from cold weather or tramps," she said.

"Mamma! it is magnificent! It is a story-book

thing! I 'm *so* happy!" and Alice danced up and down in ecstasy.

"I thought it would please you, some day," said her mother. "I kept the secret till I knew just what to do with it."

Was all this for only two weeks, — or for a month, even? It felt to Jane like a new beginning of something that was to go on into a quite different life for always. Already her changes from house to house, her dreary intervals at Mrs. Turnbull's, seemed long ago. There was a place here made for her; a thought for her in everything about it. Work? Was that what she had come for? Perhaps. Perhaps it would be for work that she should come to paradise. But in paradise, work takes other character and name. Some word sweeter than "pleasure" would stand for it in the new language.

I do not mean to detail every little thing that had to do with Jane's fortnight here; but this way in which it began was such a pretty way of its own that it needs to be represented as it was presented to her; it opens and indicates the whole spirit and expression of that which followed and surrounded her through the days.

"One thing I will say to you," Mrs. Sunderland began, as they sat down together over a basket of work. "You will know just what I mean, — and don't mean. Whatever there is here which you may notice behind my little looking-glass, unexpected or otherwise, please don't be — provoked — into explaining, in my behalf. I'd rather not be explained, if I cannot explain myself. Character is like the solar system. It has nothing to do but to go on. People will only understand what they come to, if all the secrets of the universe were chiseled out upon the rocks." Which was, perhaps a rather stately way of putting it, but Mistress Margaret Sunderland could be stately sometimes.

"Oh, I quite know," Jane answered. "It's just as true of a little bit of moss as it is of a planet." So these two met each other, and fitted to each other's thought.

If Jane ever did make common talk of anything, she would not for the world have made common talk of the things she saw and was part of for the time in Mrs. Sunderland's household. The delicate refinement of all, and the generosity that took her into it, gave it a sanctity.

"I suppose she's got more than she can finish," Mrs. Turnbull had suggested, as a final solution of the problem. This was at once a clinching of a certain theory that, chiefly through Mrs. Turnbull's observations, had sprung up in Ascutney Street, and a disposal of the contradiction to it which had at first seemed involved in Mrs. Sunderland's em-

ploy). nt of a seamstress. The theory was that
Mrs. ᴗunderland " took in work " herself. The
coming and going of certain parcels had looked
like it; and then there was a particular carriage
that came now and again of a morning, rather
early, from which either the man who drove, or a
very inconspicuous little feminine person in plain
dress who sometimes came and alighted, carried in
a basket.

" It might be fine washing, even, who knew ? "
said the Ascutney Street people. " It was n't anybody to *see* her, for it was n't a seeing hour, for
folks who would come in carriages, except on an
errand; and the girl who got out was n't a car-
riage-y looking person, either."

" It may lead to a permanency," Mrs. Turnbull
had said, in a slightly ill-used tone of sarcasm.
" She may take you in partnership."

Jane Gregory knew very well that there would
be more of this, in question and comment, when
she returned after the fortnight; and that she
should be continually provoked to mention some little quenching incidental circumstance; but now, —
and she was glad to have her own indignant pride
for her new friend strengthened by her friend's
frank word, — nothing could have drawn from her,
through provocation, artifice, or surprise, any least
betrayal.

She would not have told Mrs. Turnbull that while all the furnishings of the little house which had been observable in the landing from the wagons, or patent at windows, were of the simplest, there were other things that had come invisibly in safe foldings and packings, which gave marvelous tone and finish to the home Ascutney Street knew nothing of ; things quite out of Ascutney Street experience or imagination. She would not have said that while " there was not a woolen carpet in the house," there were rugs of indescribable softness and richness in the bedrooms, a superb tiger-skin with ivory claws stretched out before the settee-like sofa of wickerwork in one parlor, and that in the other was a bear-skin like a snowdrift. She might not have been able to state that a great, beautiful etching of a Madonna upon one wall was an Overbeck ; or a painting of a tiny, lovely bit of wood-glade, with two rabbits alert and listening with slender, erected ears that seemed to say "Hark ! " like uplifted fingers, — whence you felt at once the gesture of the uplifted finger must have somehow grown, — and quivering with the spring that was presently to take them flashing away into a thicket from some as yet far-off alarm was a real Landseer. She would not have told of the children's " moon," or the fair, white sculpture of the Persephone, that rested on the only bit of

velvet or fine upholstery stuff in the room, a gar-
net-covered bracket; she would not have counted
as upholstery a table-cover or two that were like
woven pictures; nor spoken of the books that filled
from floor to ceiling a plain set of dark-stained
shelves.

Of the life they lived there, it would have been
of no use to speak; people must live a piece of such
to know it. The very questions of the children
were of a range and realm that the mere good-
clothes - wearing, scrupulous - card - leaving, lunch-
spreading and lunch - eating round had never
touched; that it was too busy with its own labo-
rious following and striving to reach up to.

They played out whole fairy-tales in the white
room and the rooms adjoining, which were the children's for their sleep and sport; and the long L-passage and the outer platform, with the garden stairs
leading to the shade and pleasantness of the small
but pretty grounds, served them for space and
scenery enough.

Mrs. Sunderland was as happy and as earnest
as Alice and Rick; she said she liked them to live
out their little imaginations, and represent in action
what had so pleased them in fancy. To them it
was realization: and to realize one's ideals, even if
beginning only with nursery fables, was the way to
live. It would lead to actualization of theories,

perhaps, in after times, which otherwise might remain useless day-dreams forever. For this very
reason she but slightly approved of exhibited the-
atricals : these were the formalizing less of the
thing than the shadow ; they beguiled into self-
consciousness ; whereas the genuine " be-ing," as
the children called it, their favorite characters, and
the " doing " of their deeds, was a self-surrender
to that which they ardently delighted in and admired.

With all their pretty make-believes, Jane
thought there were never little people so honestly
and simply real, as the two little Sunderlands.

" The great mistake in all living," said Mrs.
Sunderland to her, " is the keeping of two separate
selves : one that would be, and one that is. There
is always some way of uniting the two."

" Do you think so ? " asked Jane, surprised.
" There is something that is stronger than would
or will, I 'm afraid. *Must* treads both down."

" Make *must* serve your own turn, then," said
Mrs. Sunderland.

" Men may do that," said Jane meekly. " They
make the world suit them, or turn it upside down.
Girls have a hard time."

" Are you there, little one ? " asked Mrs. Sunderland, with a laugh. " Better steer round that
snag ; let the iron double-bows run against that.

My dear ! " she broke forth in fresh, serious earnest, " *boys* have a hard time ! They 're getting so
dreadfully shoved aside. They 're pushed away
from behind the counters, and out of the profes-
sions. I think it 's a great shame. Why, a young
man can't marry, nowadays, until some young
woman, I suppose, has laid up a prudent compe-
tence, enough to support a husband, and comes and
asks him. And by the time they might come, they
know better ; there is n't any motive. A *man* can't
make a *home*, while the woman does the other
thing ! I 've a feeling on this subject, Jane ; I 've
got kinsmen, — and friendsmen, — and I know
how horrid it is for them. They would want nice
wives, of course ; and they — Well — there 's poor
old Hans gone out West, away from everybody
he likes and belongs to, to ride round among the
ranches, and get caught in the blizzards. Why
don't these enterprising women do that, if they 're
so equal to everything? Men have to take the
rough, it seems, and make the places, and women
are to come in as fast as they 're smoothed out, and
fill all up, and drive on the poor fellows, that ought
to be some of their husbands, to more wilderness,
like the hunted aborigines ! "

" Women can't all marry," said Jane.

" No, of course they can't, under such circumstances. It 's because the men can't. I don't say

it's all their doing, — just in this way; but that's part of it; and between the dolls and the drivers, it's done. And then, where the men are n't angels, it comes back upon the women, and there are the poor unspeakables."

"Still as things are, we have got to work, or starve, or — come to the unspeakable."

"Work, — yes; you're in the right line, my dear; but the other two, — no! there are homes yet; and they want more women in them. Daughters don't stay; or if they do, it is n't much for home, only for headquarters; literally, a place to put their heads in when they are n't in their bonnets. They've got the boom, and they're off for outside careers and causes. This is where the change and the compensation come in, and will keep the world round, after all. It's a game of puss-in-the-corners, and the wise pussies will slip into the corners, by the firesides and the mending-baskets and the cradles. You're all wanted there, Jane Gregory, and you're not wanted in the crowd and hustle."

"I wonder if women could n't do something in the new places," said Jane thoughtfully.

"Out there among the blizzards? Why, yes; and as fast as they get there, they do it, the women's part of it, — and that way has to be often, to be sure, a piece of the men's; but for the first clearing, the very roughest, the men generally go ahead alone. After the families begin, there begin to be pussy corners, you know, too; even in log cabins."

" I don't see how the families do begin," said Jane.

" A few go in families at the start, of course; some leave their families in the old places for a while, and fetch them when they 've chopped the woods a little, or ploughed up a bit of prairie; and then there are the towns that are laid out and settled up all in the lump, like the sentences children read without spelling. I never considered it very systematically; but that 's the way we hear about it. And — Oh, the railroads, of course; they are like rockets with lines to them, fired off from point to point over the breaks and chasms, and bridging the way for the crowd, that will go wherever it sees a bridge. Oh, yes; settling the country is done by the big job, now, but it does n't make new country into old home, for all that; and it 's hard for a long time for a man like my — like — Hansel."

Mrs. Sunderland felt a sudden little mental twitch when she came to the name that before had been so quick upon her lips. She had nearly said something else, something much more fully explanatory; and then it occurred to her that she would not. Not at all in any wild, remote, impossible reference to Jane; such never entered her sensible head; only as it concerned herself. Something inclined her, in the attitude things had taken with her in Ascutney Street, not to make manifest even to Jane, quite yet, the least bit of her personal and social links; names and relationships open up a good deal. "Sunderland" might happen to be anybody's name; but if the whole of Doctor Hansel's, and its connection with herself, were as this and that set together, they would, to a great many people, give the key to the whole story which she meant for a while to have the fun of keeping to herself.

Not one of these small Ascutney Street men of the modern little multitudinous business world, but would have heard, at least traditionally, of the stately old mercantile firm of Griffith and Sunderland, that was great on the wharf and the exchange long before Ascutney Street was even a cross footpath over the country fields, or ever an "hourly" omnibus plodded from that precinct to the city. And nobody, who knew by the merest hearsay of present general society, but could tell you that the Griffiths and Sunderlands had so married back and forth in two or three generations, besides reaching matrimonially into other strong parallels, that these stood as at the head of a list, the very mention of any single family of which suggested a whole clan

and history of social power, having its roots ı.
least three great metropolitan centres. It did nc
matter, in individual cases, whether the money
power were there or not; of course many a young
Griffith or Sunderland had his own way to make,
as Margaret said; and probably it came all the
harder upon them in the matter of starting new
centres and planting new homes.

All this parenthesis is ours; it was but a flash in
Margaret Sunderland's mind as she spoke.

"Is it Doctor Hansell who is the children's uncle Hans?" Jane asked quite innocently.

"They call him so," answered the duplicit Margaret.

CHAPTER VI.

"You need not thank me so meekly, dear old Hans, for my tumultuous letter-writing to you; it is my only safety-valve. But then you always were my steam-escape, you know, — the only one I can puff off all my half-condensed sublimations to. How queer it is that nobody seems to realize — as we always did, since the days we traveled off to the old witch-fairy's sugar-candy-and-gingerbread house together — that all we do in this world is to live out some fable or other; and that 'only a fable' means only a thing factable. You need n't laugh at my English words or my Latin derivation. I 've looked it out and don't care. It 's all one in creation, to speak and to do. You were half right and two thirds wrong — and that also is an anti-common-sense possibility — in shaking your head at my experiment in coming here to Ascutney Street, and trying life alongside a different row of people from those I had been accustomed to, and who, I insist upon it, had a most limiting and re-pressing influence upon one whole side of me that was getting paralyzed and withered in consequence of the cramp and useless tying-down. I *knew* I was right at the start, and in the leading motive, — to do something at my end that should correspond to what brave old Rick was doing at his, and so the sooner, perhaps, make the two ends meet again. I knew I was right in leasing Bay Hill, and getting out of the expenses there. It was no use for Rick to say, ' You can remain as you are; I don't see any need to alter things essentially for you here,' when I knew the money it would take would be just so much out of what he was going off to the opposite meridian to get together again and make up his losses with; just so much time lengthened out — days for dollars — in our separation. For the way of living involves so much, — more than just the housekeeping accounts from month to month; it settles the whole principle of plan and calculation and necessity in the general and for the future. I knew he would not come back until he could feel he need never go again ; and I wanted, in case of disappointment or break in health, or any trouble here apart from money, in which we *must* have each other, that there should be a kind of living established and proved that he could come right back to. I wanted to find out that we might do without paraphernalia. Besides all this I had a curiosity. I wanted to take the chance to dip a

while into a different piece of the story ; to get near
to something simpler, — something more primitive
and neighborly.   I thought I should like to live in
a quiet little country street, with people who did
not ride in their own carriages, or give grand re-
ceptions, but knew each other's little ins and outs,
and were especially sympathetic with the outs.

"There 's just where I missed it. They don't. I
plunged myself, unbidden and without introduc-
tion, right into the midst of the fiercest kind of an
aristocracy ; aristocracy, I was going to say, in the
making ; only I fancy it is not precisely the genuine process.   It is rather aristocracy in the poten-
tial ; and which takes upon itself the indicative.

" Do you believe, they *would n't let me in ?* I 've
been here six months, and not a creature has called
upon me.   They look at me over the fences, and
spy me out and guess at me, and decide that I am
not their sort, and that the bars are not to be let
down.   So I have hidden myself up more than
ever.   And the fun of it — is even beyond what
the experiment would have been ! I never guessed
before how easy it was to hide and be forgotten.
Why, you have only to slip out of your place for a
moment, with whatever slight pretext, and — pro-
vided you have done nothing to bring the police
after you — there are n't half a dozen persons to
bother about you, or care whether you ever turn

up or not, till you choose to put yourself in evidence once more. 'Out of town' is all there needs to be said about it. 'Gone a journey,' — it does n't matter whether five miles or five thousand, since you 're off, — and people have turned round to the next thing. I would have gone out West with you, if that had n't been really too wild a notion with the children; but here, only as far west as Chesterbury, I am just as secure. Even if I run up against anybody in a town shop, I need only say, 'Down from the country on an errand or two,' and they let me go again, both out of sight and out of mind, with the most Barkis-y willingness! Of course I owe much immunity to the fact that Rick has gone to the far Indian seas to patch up the hole in his fortune, and that we sold the town house and the ponies and a carriage or two, before he left. Doubtless when some of the kin reassemble within easy drive after their scattered summerings, it will change the aspect. A few more carriages coming and going will perhaps open wider the curious eyes to a kind of enlightenment they can take in. The fun will then be to see what they can consistently do about it.

"Do you know, Hansel, why the knight's move is the most puissant on the chessboard? It is the move of courtesy and valor; so it carries strength and privilege. The mightiest majesty cannot budge at all, of course, except to edge itself from a threatened intrusion; the castles — the great solid established powers and orders — go up and down their perpendiculars and horizontals, and bear tremendously on whatever is precisely in their way; the bishops, and other clergy, slide on their peculiar diagonals, seeming to avoid the rigidities of rank, but maintaining their own; the queen, — ah! she indeed may vary with the subtle dominance of the suave oblique, the dignified limit of the direct, but her weakness is that she cannot, after all, for whatever emergency, break out of range or confuse her lines. See what the knight, the free noble, does! He alone leaps the boundary! He only can take two steps on his own road and one off at the same time upon the path of his neighbor; or one step off from self and the conventional, and two alongside in fellowship upon the next parallel. Over heads, across barriers, he springs and alights as he will, and as he is wanted. It is he who solves the problems and defies the hindrances; and he never jumbles up the game, either. Hansel, chess would be awfully stupid if it were not for the knight's move!

"I only meant to write you a 'light running domestic;' but you and I always do get into the reasons of things. What I am explaining and prefacing is, that I have taken a sort of knight's

jump myself into a next row, and found what
I should not have got precisely if I had held on
to my own particular square, or file of squares, forever. I have made friends with a most charming
little pawn, and am gently escorting her forward,
or planning to do so, step by step, out of a block
she got into, without a safe or worth-while move
for her in any direction. And you know there is
this about a pawn,—she may, under special protection, and by gently wise progression, come eventually to queen! I never thought until this minute,
what a pretty thing it is that the only piece that
has the very elements of the royal move in its own
small, unpretending, faithful, patient advances, is
the pawn!

"I have n't any special scheme for her; I do not
mean to put schemes into her head, — or even dis-
contents; I have simply got her into my home, in
her own humble capacity and use, and further into
my heart than she imagines. I do not mean to let
her go again carelessly; and I feel somehow sure
that there is something for her in the world that
maybe I can help her reach. She would n't care
to be a queen; and I don't mean place and station
for her, when I think of possible change; but some
little rule and realm that every woman likes,—at
least some little freedom and fullness of existence,
— *that* I feel like demanding for her, and wringing

out of circumstance. These Ascutney Street people have so looked down upon her! I mean just one household of them who have had her services,—for her board, I believe,—and have kept her presence with them disguised or suppressed, because they knew Ascutney Street *would* look down!

"Probably I should not have told you all this, but that I have had literally nothing else to tell of late, or to interest myself about, beyond the children's pranks; and it was a prank of theirs, indeed, that brought Jane here. She has won her way with them; Alice came upon her, as she called it, 'through the looking-glass;' which really meant, I had reason to suspect, a trespass across garden bounds into my disdainful neighbor's premises; and the child has named her—the coincidence with what I have been saying just strikes me as I write it—her White Queen.

"Maybe I have left you to suppose that I have wrapped my enthusiasm about some ordinary unbred girl of coarse service, and am trying my wand upon her, by way of turning a Cinderella into a princess, and making a coach out of a pumpkin for her to ride in. 'Altro!' If sweet, high womanliness means that, my little seamstress is a lady. She's a different 'speshoo,' as old Dobson used to say to us in her descriptive comments on Australian natural history.

"Do not think, either, that I am uncomfortable here, or desolate, or repenting my bargain. I have got more experience, and some better things, than I came for; the house and garden are pretty and nice; the children are happy, for they fetched their fairyland with them; Primrose comes to see me, on her way to and from the trains, where she leaves or meets her husband, and brings me apricots and roses and grapes from Edgemere; I have Rick and you to write to; and I don't even contemn — I only watch, as a specimen in the grub condition — Ascutney Street.

"Now I want another long letter from the wilds. I don't care if it *isn't* a ranch country, or mines and gulches, or a tornado track; all these things *are* west of the Mississippi, and so are you; and I'm only gradually getting able to sort you out and set you apart. Has your old Swedish woman learned to pronounce her *j's*, or got her tongue round all the consonants in the 'Griffith' yet? or does she still despair of that, and call you 'Dhocdhor Yan,' and does she make yam, and yems, and yonnycake for you, and open yars of yinyer, when the yudye rides over at tea-time? And *did* her currant yelly yell?

"I'm very peaceful about your having her, dear old Hans; and the photograph of the little long, low house is lovely, with the natural park-like surroundings of soft sweeping turf and the far shadows among the groups of lordly old black walnuts! Sunnywater is a picture and a poem, in the very name; but I can't trust altogether to that for you; and I do hate to think of those long rides out to the farms, and the winter storms, and the break-neck road to the fort, and only Mrs. Knutzen and her boy Bap for you to come home to!"

HANSEL TO GRETEL.

"Don't worry, little woman, about what I have to come home to, when you keep me company your-self with such budgets as that I have just spent half my evening with. And as to what I go out to, you simply can't think what the glorious differ-ence is between a rush over the prairie with a fairly beaten bridle-path to follow, or even a scramble down the bluff and a transit by the cable ferry to the opposite scramble up again, and the tame ways of crowded civilization, hanging on to straps in horse-cars, timing trains, or driving along macad-amized thoroughfares in a continuous procession that never passes a given point in any number of hours together. Why, I never got *out*, before, in all my life, until I came here! and I think I am like the genie that got out of the bottle. Now I have fairly stretched myself, I don't believe I shall ever get back again, — to stay, at any rate.

" The joke of your supposing that going to Ascutney Street — the last little adaptation of Queen-
Anne-to-the-million in pretentious demand and
supply for modern measures and patterns of living
— would bring you into some sweet, arcadian
simplicity ! Of course the simplicity all went there
with yourself, like the children's fairyland, and
was speedily disenchanted into a very disgusted
enlightenment. I am glad, however, that you are
not wholly disheartened or desolate ; you would be
pretty sure to be preventing somebody else from
being so wherever you were.

" As to your chess parable, I can add a simili-
tude to those you have so ingeniously fitted. Does
it occur to you what the doubled pieces mean ?
That there is a king's side and a queen's side to the
affairs of life ? Yours is the feminine chivalry,
the knight's move with the womanly power; there
remains to be made a reinforcing of the position
by the K. Kt. And where is he, to be on your
part for your white pawn ? If you can bring him
forward, my lady, I think you may have done your
work.

" But these little pawns with the queen's impulse
in them have a hard time getting across the board,
even among their friends. I have caught glimpses
of such in my ways among all sorts; and I know
just the kind of ' sweet, high womanliness,' without

its fair chance, that you mean. And yet, — you women of the step above, — are you always willing to make real room for them, a place beside you that would need no patronage? I wonder what you would say to me, for instance, Gretel, if I were to take a knight's jump somewhere, and lead a little white pawn toward the front?"

When Margaret got thus far in Doctor Hansel's letter, I am bound to say she made a long pause and catechized herself, and I am afraid she did not come out from the catechizing quite satisfied with the lesser self to which the nobler put the test questions. I am afraid that she was not quite ready that Doctor Hansel should make that knight's move. "At any rate," she said, taking up the letter from her lap with a long breath, "he is away out there. One need not trouble about it yet awhile. He won't pick up a *red* pawn, — nor a black one. He's a white knight." She did not fancy the white pawns were especially plenty at Sunnywater.

The rest of the letter she read aloud afterward to Rick and Alice; and Jane Gregory heard it.

"I would like to have had you and the children with me up the river on a holiday I have just had. I don't often go out of instant reach of my work; but I had no especial cases, and there is a good fellow out here on a prospect for a practice, whom I have half a mind to go shares with myself, in a circuit I can hardly swing round to now, and that will double up its population in ten years' time. Anyhow, I took this run — went up on one of the government boats with an inspecting party under Major Griggs. There were half a dozen pleasant men, and two or three ladies. We went where the Indian summer comes from. All along the river lands was that lovely haze like gold mist, and the trees and creepers were just beginning to kindle up. You have no idea how a creeper does grow, when it has only one thing to cling to. If I were a versifier, I would save that to make a poem of. But the poem was there, with a thousand others. You will see a tall elm, with a trunk column as round as a fair Doric, running straight up all by itself sixty feet before it throws out its tent of boughs ; and a vine starting at its roots has laid every shoot and leaf close down upon the bark, knowing right well there is nothing else near to fling out for ; and so climbing and clinging and facing itself all the time toward the light, it has fitted a perfect, unbroken mosaic of foliage to the tree-pillar. Above, where it gets to the branches, the streamers and festoons have their way, and the whole splendid thing is alive with breath and motion in the high blue air. The colors, breaking out here and there on single leaf or tips and clusters, are like jewels among green enamel. Fancy the whole tree incrusted, as it will be soon, with such a fretwork of gems, and then imagine a colonnade of such trees just far enough from each other to keep their single perfection, and you have one of the variety of pictures that this up-river, lazy stroll, in shallow, uncertain waters, gave and suggested to us, with sufficient lingering before each point to make it thoroughly a study and possession.

"The solitude of these river stretches between the towns is wonderful. The channel changes make the farm borders so uncertain on the water-lines, that a man may have acres of plantation one year that are all under the river next; and of course they build their houses away back in safer places. You see nothing of habitation; when the boat wants fresh eggs or butter, a yawl is sent off to a landing, and the men go up country a mile or more for a supply. Fancy the sunsets in this width of stillness, when the hazy air turns crimson and pink; and the twilights and the moonlight nights!

"I know it; there's where the romance might come in. But somehow, I think romance would have interrupted. Chatter did, often. I think almost any kind of talk, measured against that grand quietness, would have sounded small; the distance was hardly appreciable, in such contrast, between the light conversation of the upper deck and the chaff and chuckle of the roustabouts down below.

"There were two pretty young women on board, but there was n't any " — ("H'm! nonsense!" Margaret interpolated. The next words really were "White Queen.")

"An incident happened one day, however, which reminded me of a glimpse I did once get" — ("H'm — h'm! I believe I 've lost my place," said Mistress Margaret, glancing on and returning. "Ah, here it is") . . . — "steaming up finely along an open run of deep water, making the best time we could to reach the furthest point of our trip before night. There was a fresh wind, almost directly in our faces; we were on deck, enjoying the exhilaration of progress after so much dawdling; when for an instant the breeze rose to a gust, and two hats went off, whirling down and across stream, and finally lodging among the weeds and osiers of a broad marsh. One belonged to an officer, and one was a young lady's. There was a good deal of fun, of course; the girl was very pretty, and her hair got loose and flew picturesquely about her face; she behaved nicely enough, but rather as if she enjoyed it; and afterward there was some to-do about turning a spare soft felt of the major's, with twisting and ribboning, into a feminine headgear, that was successfully effected, and the thing sported with the least little air of pleased distinguishment, during the rest of the voyage.

"I'll tell Alice of the other thing — like and unlike — that I saw once. It was a great deal harder for the girl, for it was on a railroad train, full of passengers, going into the city. The hat blew off as she stood upon the platform, just as the cars left a way station; she had to go into the carriage and sit down, bareheaded; and she did it just as simply and as quietly as if — she had had a half yard's height of bows and plumes overhead to keep her in countenance, instead of only some light, beautiful rolls of sunny-colored hair, and a few soft, wavy tips or short locks that touched her forehead and temples like the fringy edges of a little bird's feathers. She looked troubled, but she did not let even that appear, very much. She never glanced to see who noticed her, or how, but slipped into the first seat and tied a scarf over her head. Somebody told the conductor, and the hat was telegraphed back for, and sent on into town not many minutes later. I happened to be near her when she recovered it and put it on; and I saw how wonderfully charming an unaffected inconspicuousness could be."

"Do you think you take that in, Alice, — the last long words and all?" Margaret asked, with a certain odd intonation, as she paused again in her reading.

" Yes, I do, mamma," Alice answered positively. " I like that girl, and I don't wonder it took very particular words to tell what uncle Hans thought about her. I think uncle Hans is very noticing, don't you ? "

Jane Gregory sat perfectly motionless in a window-seat. The lamp by which Mrs. Sunderland was reading did not shine upon her, for the curtain fell partly between. A slow surge and swell of intense surprise and feeling had passed over her ; she could not have moved or spoken, yet she thrilled from head to foot.

It had come close to her again, that piece of her story ; it had joined to it something incredible ; it had so augmented and weighted itself that it could never drift away from her again into forgetfulness. Something more positive belonged to her, and yet what more of it should she ever know ?

She knew too much on her side, little Jane Gregory. To this Doctor Hansell, — how well she recollected the mere title by which he had been hailed in her hearing, — it was all vague and unassociated. She had lent a touch to his mental picture of an ideal ; her heart swelled that she could have done that ; but his ideal and herself, — if she could dare to think of them together, — how was it likely that ever for another instant they should coexist to him?

Mrs. Sunderland went on, resuming rather hastily her reading. Jane recollected afterward, in some mysterious way, what now fell simply on her outward ear. Inwardly, she was listening to such strange, bewildering things!

"Rick would have enjoyed seeing the snagboats that we visited at their work: great, two-beaked, clumsy things that would puff and steam down upon a tree-trunk sticking out of the water, catch it between their iron jaws like a bootjack, and yank it up, and haul it on board for firewood.

"Once, we got caught on a sandbar; it was toward the last of our down trip; stayed there a day and a half; the roustabouts went off up-shore and brought pecan nuts. It looked serious about getting off; the major was anxious to get back to headquarters, and some of us were in a hurry. We began to think of having the yawl, and rowing down to a railway landing, when at noon the second day a funny thing happened, — I'll leave the moral to you, Gretel, — another steamboat came down river, full head, a little river craft, drawing much less water than we. She saw our predicament as soon as she rounded the bend in the deep water above; we were just in the edge of the channel. The little wretch thought to give us the go-by with a flourish.   On she came, full rush, whooping, depth and width enough for her, apparently; but, behold you, the heave and swell she brought with her rolled beautifully under our keel, lifted us up, and carried us sweeping over, while in our very wake she drifted exactly into our old place, and stuck there fast. As we steamed away, roustabouts shouting and whistle screaming, they were getting poles in rig on board the other for working off. 'They'll do well enough,' said the major nonchalantly. 'Small enough to swim anywhere.' Suggesting that as a timely aphorism, I'll shut up."

"I'm so glad I was n't on board that mean little steamboat!" Rick exclaimed, as his mother stopped.

"Rick thinks he really was on the other, with uncle Hans," Alice remarked superiorly. "Mamma, what is an aphorism?"

"A pithy saying; something said in a few words that means a great deal."

"I think uncle Hans is a pretty pithy man sometimes," was Alice's meditative comment, as she buttoned her doll's nightgown.

"Are you tired?" Mrs. Sunderland asked, turning to Jane.

"On the contrary — I was thinking," Jane replied, gathering herself back slowly, "what a different thing living is — among live people."

" Ascutney Street folks ? "

" Live and lively may be quite distinct," said Jane.

" Are you two talking aphorisms ? " inquired Miss Alice.

CHAPTER VII.

I COULD tell you a mere story in three paragraphs, or even Cæsarean phrases: they met; they wooed; they married; — she was here, in this strait; that happened; she did thus and so; she came out there. But that would not be telling you the things that are the complexion of life and character. Complexion is general hue and aspect, but it is made up of a thousand peculiarities and combinations of texture and color. I should not care two straws what eventually became of Jane Gregory, if I could not enter in beforehand to what made Jane Gregory just what she was.

Her days with Mrs. Sunderland were crucial ones; they brought to light much; they influenced and determined much. In this new action upon her of circumstances, her past stood clearer, what it had bred in her more apparent. She was hardly less a study to herself, — or a re-presentation, — than she was to her friend.

The soreness and the weariness that she had felt, in contact with small pretense and an unvarying iteration of petty, external routine and detail, came

" Au all her expression of herself, and in her con-
dence that answered to unwonted interest and
sympathy. It was plain that much of this soreness
had grown to be morbid, and needed to be broken
up and worn off; it interfered with the highest
and most essential things; it cramped hope and
spirit, and even faith, as well as daily motive.

" Pretense," said Mrs. Sunderland, one day, in
reply to something Jane had spoken with her peculiar gentle bitterness that was not distilled of
noxiousness, but rather of an honest wholesome-
ness, like the pungency of the meek, sturdy little
camomile flower, — " pretense may be true or
false."

" *Pretense!* True ? "

" Yes ; or why do we emphasize ' false pretenses ' ?
It is simply the taking hold of beforehand ; and to
apprehend and appropriate a true thing beforehand
is just what we live for."

Alice sat by, catching such bits as she could, as
usual. " Monkeys are pre-hensile," she volunteered,
with learned reference to natural history.

" Very much so, in a certain way," said her
mother, laughing ; " that is partly illustrative of
what we are talking about; people seizing hold and
lifting themselves up by their meaner capacities
only. Monkeys drop that, it is to be supposed,
when they get rid of their tails, and begin to de-
velop their brains."

"Mrs. Sunderland," Jane said suddenly, "it is why I left off going to church! It seemed — almost all of it — like make-believe. I tried different sorts: in some they were always turning the Bible over and over, settling and unsettling things — ideas — *about* it; not looking right straight *into* it, at all; just as people turn a letter over and over, and guess about the date and the postmark and the handwriting, and never break the seal to see what it says to them. And in others, they had got out of it — or with it — something that they had worked up into a set scheme or ceremony, just as the children of Israel made the golden calf out of all the earrings and ornaments, and fell down and worshiped that, while Moses was up in the mountain with the Lord. It was exactly the same that it is in society; people worship style, and they worship *church !* And then you read such things, and hear people say them, who won't worship, and who are outside of the whole. Moses did n't write his books, and John did n't write his; they explain everything except how anything got written at all, until you feel as if nothing ever did, and nothing ever truly happened."

"My dear child! you *have* got your foot in the tangle! Just take hold of this, and be sure it is true: when we have got the least little bit of the word of God — that is everywhere — into our hearts; when He really says it to us in ourselves, — we shall feel what it is in the things other hearts have learned from Him. The Bible is full of these things; and that is how we must come to know them. That is the grain of mustard-seed the whole church grows up from; *that's* why the birds sing in the branches!"

"But people *don't* begin at the heart, they don't *grow* into it; they are n't native birds; they are strange, common, coarse fowls that only crowd in, and roost; and they break the branches down!"

"They have only got as far as Ascutney Street yet," said Mrs. Sunderland. "It is the court of the Gentiles."

"But will Ascutney Street ever come to anything else? It is so satisfied."

"That is the hindrance, all through everything. Ascutney Street is so apt to be satisfied, and to stay. It likes to rest in an effect; and to hide, or to ignore, the real. It slips over, covers up, the want, the hope, the struggle, the hard work, and assumes the thing is done. If one could catch them at it, in their hearts or in their kitchens, and make them understand actual values, and not be false-faced or ashamed!"

"How clear you see! That is just it. I have often admired behind the scenes; the work, the capability, that were real. I 've said to myself, —

and almost right out, — Oh, why *are n't* you proud of, content with, *that?*"

"Let's set a trap, Jane, and catch somebody! Who do you think would be easiest?"

Jane laughed. "I don't know them much, of course. I've been kept out of that. But I should say the nicest of them all is Miss Rickstack. I suppose the nicest would take your sort of bait the quickest."

"The nicest did," returned Mrs. Sunderland concisely. "But Miss Rickstack, — which is she? What does she do?"

"She does everything. She lives all alone. She irons her clothes, and shakes her rugs after dark, and has a beautiful garden. She is just wild after flowers."

"Well, my trap will be to watch my chance. Chances are always happening; if you have your mind set on a thing, there'll be a way to it. That's what the proverb means."

"The 'will and the way'? I thought that was just 'you could if you really wanted to.'"

"All the same. But I mean that the chances drift to the will, — where there were n't any chances before. Make an object of anything and see."

Three days later, it happened just as Mrs. Sunderland had said. At bedtime, an express wagon stopped at her gate. A package for Mrs. Sunderland, which she had expected; another left with it, which was not hers at all, but which the driver in his hurry had glanced and guessed at, in the light of the street lamp. It was directed to Miss R. L. Rickstack. The identity of the first two initials, and a big whiplash loop to the standard of the " R," with the running likeness in the surname, in its equal number of tall letters, had sufficed for the blunder. It was a box from Vick's, long and light and carefully put up; roots and cuttings, evidently. The man was rattling off on the avenue before the mistake was fully ascertained.

"What did I tell you?" Mrs. Sunderland demanded of Jane. "And on the same principle I *know* she will be at her ironing when I go over to-morrow morning."

"If she is, there will be a scarlet ribbon on the door-knob."

"I am not initiated. It does n't matter to me how people decorate their door-knobs. I *think* I shall go round the back way. I'm not a pushing person." Which from Mrs. Richard Lee Sunderland, who, if she pushed any way, would have to push down, was sufficiently entertaining.

It was a pretty picture she came upon the next morning at Miss Rickstack's, as she walked up the graveled path to a sheltered square porch which was really the kitchen entrance,   far more attractive than the regulation sashed door in front with its lace flutings inside the glass. As to the door-knob, and its signal, Mrs. Sunderland had slightly changed her mind, as will appear.

The secluded spot in the angle of the small building, of which the roofed platform filled one corner, was blazing with flowers, all in one raised plot, with a rim of low-banked sod. In the middle of each side a tiny footpath just reached in sufficiently to give access for the needful care to all its plants. Zinnias and asters, in clumps of garnet and gold, rose and white and purple, some shades and exquisite petalings of which were rare enough even to Margaret, — with every tint of bronze and yellow in the splendid nasturtium blooms heaping and creeping around all just inside the grass border, and tossing their tendrils and trumpets down over the edge upon the very gravel, — made a brilliantly lovely mass of color. In the midst was a little forest of sweet peas; nobody ever saw such shadings from deep to faintly delicate, or such swarms of butterfly flowers, poising and hovering and nodding from twisted columns of vinery. Opposite, by the porch step, was the low, jeweled bed of pansies, with beautiful dark velvet faces, or pale sweet silken ones, in tenderest violet, straw-color, creamy, and pure white, crowding and smiling upward. A sweet smell breathed all about; the light was lovely, the air was warm and gracious; on the porch a woman, fresh enough with plain attire of cleanest cambric, bright, open-air complexion, and nicely ordered hair, to stand among the flowers without incongruence, was busy ironing; this was Miss Rebecca Louisa Rickstack.

" I did not ring your bell; I knew by the signal you were busy; people are always busy in the morning; so I came round with my errand. You will excuse me?"

Mrs. Sunderland stopped before the platform step; she would not come further without an asking.

Miss Rickstack held her iron poised as if she were so magnetized that she could not drop it; for a breath or two she made no answer. In truth, she was mentally framing sentences explanatory of this conjuncture for Mrs. Hilum and Mrs. Turnbull; but she did not look irate or formidable, so Mrs. Sunderland went on.

" It was a mistake of the expressman; this parcel is for you, I think; it was left with one for me, late last night. I am Mrs. Sunderland, from the end cottage; you may not know."

" Oh, yes, I do; and I'm sure I beg your pardon, and I thank you very much," said Miss Rickstack, the spell upon voice and muscle relaxing, so that she set her iron safely on its stand, and her politeness into speech, as with one impulse. " Won't you come in and sit down ? "

Whether she begged pardon for the trouble the expressman had put her neighbor to, or that she had never recognized her neighbor, was not clear ; but there was a certain tone of release and pleasure in her voice, as at something she had not transgressed for, but was ready to welcome in this unconventional approach.

" May n't I stop here a minute and enjoy your flowers ? They were partly the reason, to be so far honest, that I came round by the side path. I don't think I ever saw such flowers ! "

" They are nice. I take great comfort in them, living all alone," said Rebecca Louisa, speaking tenderly of them, as if they had been children, and drawing forth a chair for her visitor's accommodation.

" And how charming to do your work out here among them ! Please don't ; I 'd rather sit here, close to the pansies, really." And Mistress Margaret placed herself upon the low wooden step, her white dress sweeping the clean, pebbly walk.

" Well, that *is* sociable ! " said Miss Rickstack, with a satisfaction ; as one might say, " This is comfort," divesting one's self of a tight shoe, or an oppressive garment. " I often wish Ascutney

Street folks did n't keep quite so much to regulation ways and times — and card-cases. I'm often lonesome, when it is n't calling hours. Do you mind if I finish this frill while my iron's hot?"

"I should be very unhappy if you let it dry; it does n't do with fine starched things." She spoke as if she might have been a laundress all her life, for any strangeness that her hostess's occupation had for her. "Ironing is pretty work; and how *beautifully* you do it!"

"It would n't answer to let some folks know I did it at all," said Miss Rickstack, with a sudden confidence.

Margaret opened her eyes with a questioning astonishment. "Really? Why, I should think you would be proud. Besides, it saves so much, in wear and tear, as well as money."

Miss Rickstack laughed. "I suppose it does, — if you count it saved when you have n't exactly got it. I save a good deal that way in carriages, and horses, and di'monds; but I don't seem to have it all!"

Then they both laughed. Miss Rickstack was evidently delighted to find some one on her own plane to whom she could unbosom herself without transgression. "I was a little in a hurry to-day, too. I'm going off to-morrow, for a fortni't, to my sister's, in Ryemouth. What in the world I'm to do with those cuttings, I don't see."

"I know something about plants," said Mrs. Sunderland. "I might set them in a box for you, and keep them watered till you come back."

"*Would* you? Why, I could n't have *asked* it —of anybody!"

"I 'd like to, very much. I 'm glad there was a mistake, and that I came."

"There ain't any mistake about *you!*" said Miss Rickstack vigorously.

"Are you sure?" The lurking mischief in the question was not in the least understood.

Miss Rickstack went into the kitchen to change her iron. When she came back, she replied, "Yes; I am. You 're straightforward. I like straightforwardness. I 'd like to be clear and above-board myself, about everything, — ironing, and sweeping, and all. But when you 're amongst folks, you have to live the most part of your life on the sly. I don't like it. It 's a great deal harder work; and it is n't free-hearted. I 'd *like* to do about everything just as I did about my teeth."

Mrs. Sunderland came very near ejaculating a repetition of the last words, with a change of pronoun. But her instinct of breeding made it impossible.

"Yes," Miss Rickstack answered to the unspoken interrogatory, just as if it had been supplied as expected.

" I 'd been a year about it, — mumble-jawed. When I got them, finally, the dentist said to me, ' There! You must n't mind if people do look at you. You 'll be strange to yourself for a while; but you must just take hold and get used to it.' Well, I went to a sewing-circle that next day; I was glad to see people, — I always am; and I suppose I smiled all round more than I was aware of. Every living soul laid down her needle, — or let her scissors gape up in the air, — or held her thread stopped short in her own teeth, — and looked at me. Then I recollected; but I made up my mind. I was just as I was going to be the rest of my during life, and I and folks had got to face it. I did n't mean to go round with a getherin'-thread in my lips, — I had n't done that when my naturals was a-failing. I took my work and sat down between Miss Caley and Mrs. Basset. That was at Ryemouth. They began to talk, and to peer and peek, sideways, tipping their heads a little, one each way, over their sewing. There was going to be a wedding in town, and they were telling that the day was just set. But la! they did n't know any more what they were talking about than you know this minute. I looked first at one and then at the other, and never tried to hide a bit; did n't even put up my pocket-handkerchief. I thought it might as well all come out at once.

They were the ones that did n't dare to be straight-out and full-faced about it ; they kept making little sharp, quick gimlety screw-tinizes ! ' Did you say it was going to be on the twentieth ? ' says I. ' Oh — 'm 'm ! ' says Miss Caley, and gave a twist, as if she was trying to unscrew the gimlet, but she could n't fairly get her eyes away. ' Twentieth ? ' says Mrs. Basset, on the other side, and she leaned down and bit off her thread, and sent a determined sort of slanting look up out of the corners of her eyes like prying with a crowbar ; ' N–o, — it is n't the twentieth ; it 's the twenty-second.' I smiled as much as ever I could, first one way and then the other, to treat 'em both alike. ' Why did n't you say the twenty-*tooth ?* ' said I. And after that I had my new property to myself. When people know all they can know, they 'll let you alone."

Mrs. Sunderland came home, sat down in the white room with Jane, and laughed with tears in her eyes. " She 's bewitching ! I 'm intimate with her. And she 's going away for a ' fortni't ' ! So *un*-fortnit for me ! "

Jane was going away for a fortnight also, to keep an old promise of " fall work," and then to return for some odd days with Mrs. Turnbull, also promised. " But after," said Mrs. Sunderland, " we 'll all begin where we left off ! "

After a fortnight ! When a day or an hour can

set us forward to a life's length from what we left off with so confidently! Things were to happen in this fortnight.

Mrs. Sunderland had something on her mind. A step, — whether to take it or not; and she was not clear precisely as to what hindered her.

It would be good for the children; just what she had needed for them. And good for the girl? She had thought so. Why was she doubting?

Margaret was not fond of temporary expedients or relations; she always wanted things to last, at least to be begun with an intent and promise of lasting. Now this was so good, — so much better than the common, — that it was becoming evident to her that it would last, if it began. How much was she willing to be responsible for, in the girl's own behalf, or in connection with herself, under all possible circumstances? How far would she risk setting in train whatever might follow such transplanting of precisely this sort of young woman, with her contrarieties of nature and environment, her antagonisms of capacity and place? She was too fine a creature to be repressed, of too tender and sweet a womanliness to be crushed. What might come to her, and how might she, Margaret Sunderland, stand affected, in the new openings, the contingent occurrences, the — providence of God? Was that it, after all? Was she undertaking, in these ponderings of the future, what ʟ longed only to omniscient counsels? What, then, definitely and simply, did belong to her?

To do the good deed, — to brighten a life, — to "lend" into it — as her little Alice was so fond of saying — things that were the possession of her own, and to gain in return a fresh, genuine friendship, a help of love and intelligence in her motherly cares, and the safe contented consciousness that she had not passed by on the other side, when she came, *as she journeyed*, — not out of her way, or in a purposed straining, — to where the chance of service was? And then just to leave all that might grow of it to the Lord? It did not take a woman like Margaret Sunderland long to settle a question with herself when it had got thus far; it was no longer with herself only.

There were certain things she did not as yet know; perhaps that was well; if she had known them, they would have been a part of what she was bound intelligently to consider. She did the thing she felt she had received her order to do. She asked Jane if, when her present engagements were ended, she would return to herself; would make a part of her family, take her little children in personal charge, and resume, under more favoring conditions, the work of teaching for which she had been fitted.

When Jane heard that, she just burst into tears. "Why, Mrs. Sunderland!" was all she could say in reply.

"Then you will come, my dear?" Mrs. Sunderland said, with an ignoring of the emotion more sweetly tactful than any spoken soothing or assurance. It calmed Jane instantly with its quiet, natural assumption. The thing was in a moment no longer too good to be true, but so good that it had to be true.

"Why, surely I will!" she said. "And I will be as much to you as I am capable of being. And when I cannot be all you want, I will thank you and go away."

"We will let by-and-by's be by-and-by's," answered Margaret to that.

CHAPTER VIII

AT the end of the fortnight Jane came back to Ascutney Street.

Reaching Mrs. Turnbull's house at about the tea hour, she passed directly to her room to take off her things, and make no delay in presenting herself in time, possibly, to be of assistance.

On her table lay a little note. She knew already, as she knew distinctly everything of Mrs. Sunderland's that had thus far come under her observation, the strong, delicate, characterized hand. She opened it eagerly.

"This has been sulphur-smoked: no one need fear; but do not come to my house at present. Little Rick has diphtheria.   M. G. S."

Jane put on her hat which she had just laid off. She took some things quickly from her hand-bag, put them away, and replaced them with others from a bureau drawer. She wrote two pencil lines at the foot of Mrs. Sunderland's note, and carried it into Mrs. Turnbull's room, where she placed it open on the dressing-table. Mrs. Turnbull's voice was at that moment to be heard from the front piazza.

What Jane had written was this : —

"Mrs. Sunderland needs me. I am sorry, but will come to you as soon as I can safely.

JANE."

Three minutes afterward, she had passed across the garden, gone up the outer stairs, and entered the white room. There she found Alice. Aunty had gone to fetch some supper for the child. Mrs. Sunderland, with a trained nurse, was isolated in her own room, taking care of Rick.

"Why, Queen!" cried Alice.

"Yes, I've come," said Jane. "I am going to take care of you."

The outside door opened again; the other was fast, battened with cotton. An excellent thing that garden stair was now. Aunty entered.

"The Good save us!" she ejaculated. "You here! Be right off, jest as quick as you can. We 've got diptheery."

"I know it. I have come to stay. I 'll take care of Alice. You will have your hands full."

Aunty sat down, the little tray on her lap. She did not speak for fully a minute. Things vibrated in her mind with anxious force. But at the minute's end, she broke forth.

"Well! — you 're here, — and I suppose you 've done it! They won't want you anywhere else now, most likely. If I 'd had it to *think* of, — I should have been every which way in my mind to once. I'm clear thankful to you, — though you'd no business to 'a' come. We can sail straight now, — and I can't stand bein' wee-wawed! Alice, child, here's crab-apple jell to your bread and butter."

It was a strange life there in the white room for many days after that.

Nothing but the most rigid measures would satisfy Mrs. Sunderland. Now that Jane was come, even Aunty, who held the most remote and guarded communication possible with the hospital quarter of the little house, was forbidden to approach them. All that they needed was placed upon the outer stair, everything scalded or fumigated that was used by them, — and Jane herself did all the fetching in and out. Aunty had the kitchen work; the parlors were unvisited; a tin cake-box, rigged by its handles to a cord and pulley, went up and down between an upper and lower window with supplies, and was kept cleansed for every transit. No risk had been run, since the nature of the disease had declared itself; and yet who could say what subtle death-atom might have been borne earlier, through some unthought-of channel, or even from first causes, to lurk and work in the atmosphere of the pure, secluded little room, or might

float now, despite all watchfulness, in its horrible
minuteness and invisibility, through the stirring
and enfolding air, to be caught into the dear little
breath and life for whose security they fought
blindly with the unknown? At any moment it
might reveal itself in ghastly triumph. And Jane
knew all that, and had known it when she came.
Mrs. Sunderland had sent to Jane a verbal message
through her two assistants, which was called up by
Aunty from the garden, and which lay warm at
Jane's heart all through the time of anxious quar-
antine.

"Tell her she is an angel of God," had been the
word of love and thanks. Jane treasured it, in inmost humility and joy.

"I am so *glad* to be here!" she had sent back,
written on a bit of paper.

"An angel is but a messenger," she said to herself; "the greatest, or the least little one of all,
even." And she lifted up her heart, showing it,
with the joy in it, as the priest shows the offering
at the altar, to Him who had sent — no, *brought*
her here, in wonderful close tenderness of giving.

Little letters went down on the tray and up in
the tin box to the mother from Alice, with word
from Jane as to the child's happiness and well-
being; no scrap of anything tangible returned, but
answers by word of mouth traveled back to them,

few in syllables, and such as could not be changed or forgotten on the way, so full and alive they were with that which impelled them.

A card was hung to the bell-knob at the front entrance, with the one word upon it in clear, large characters, which was sufficient to turn any casual comer aside.

On the third day of Jane's stay, however, somebody came up the steps to the piazza, just after the doctor's chaise had driven away.

Miss Rickstack had got home, had discovered the signs of illness, and had heard from the horrified and even resentful neighbors that that queer woman had brought diphtheria among them. "A thing that was never heard of in Ascutney Street before!" they said indignantly.

"*Death* has n't been heard of in Ascutney Street yet, — please the Lord it may n't be now," said Miss Rickstack. "But it 's got to come, all the same, as sure as there 's livin' folks here for it to come to. We 're dyin' flesh, and no other kind, if we *have* got Dutch doors and Queen-Anne winders!"

And Rebecca Rickstack threw up all her Ascutney Street allegiance at that rebellious instant, and within the hour marched obliquely across the way, in as direct a line as she could make, to the marked dwelling, which every one else passed by with holden breath and on the other side.

At the door she paused and bethought herself. "Maybe the best thing I can do will be to help with the child that is n't sick. And before I mix myself up, I 'll find out."

Saying this in her own mind, she descended the steps again, and made a circuit of the house around through the side ground and the garden. "If I can't see anybody at the winders, I 'll go home and write a note," she continued, in her mental reflections.

But at the farther end, as she came out from among the screening shrubbery, she caught sight of Jane and Alice upon the platform at the head of the garden stairs, sitting there in two chairs, with a little table between them.

"I ain't the least mite afraid," she called out instantly and eagerly. "But I 've come to see what use I can be. If I can do anything to help nurse, I 'll take right hold, any minute. And I know about nursin', too. But if it 's something else that 's wanted, I 'll keep out of t' other and do that. See here," she went on, her idea and purpose developing as she spoke, "you tell Mrs. Sunderland that she 's welcome to me and my house for all we 're worth. There 's nobody to be hurt there but the cat; and 't ain't ketchin' to cats, I don't believe. You say I 'd admire to have you bring the little girl right over, and stay as long as you

like. 'T would be a real good change for her, and
she must be lonesome. I 've got lots of things that
I had fifty years ago, when I was little, and some
twenty years older than that, that was my mother's.
I always liked them best. She 'd be amused with
'em, and I ain't forgot how to play with 'em,
neither. Maybe you don't know who I am. I 'm
Miss Rickstack, and I live over at The Crocus."

After Miss Rickstack got started, both ideas and
expressions flowed; the whole thing took beautiful
and convincing shape in thought and word at once;
and was more convincing to the listener for being
thus instant to herself.

Jane spoke as soon as she had a chance. She
came down the steps as she did so. "Indeed I will
let Mrs. Sunderland know. You are as kind as
you can be. Yes, — I know quite well who you
are," — she came up to the good lady as she went
on, and held out both hands to her; "and if Mrs.
Sunderland approves, I think it would be nice for
Alice to have the change. Not altogether, — I
did n't mean that; but to come sometimes. I will
send up word at once."

"And you 'll give my love to her, and I hope
the little boy — it 's a little boy, is n't it? — is getting on well? You have Dr. Escue, have n't you?
Dr. Rescue, I call him. He 'll do all anybody can,
and what most folks can't." She shook Jane's two

hands, which she had kept in a firm grasp, and having said her say, albeit somewhat lengthily, made her movement to go, only pausing with the real question in her face which she had merged with the rest of her inquiry in such intricate fashion.

" Rick is a strong child," Jane answered; " there is good encouragement, I believe; but he is not out of danger yet. To-morrow we shall know more."

" I 'll come again to-morrow. Or to-night, or any time, if you want anybody. Or I 'll stay at home and be ready for you and " —

" Alice ? " Jane supplied the name with a heartful tone.

" Yes, and Alice. Just take The Crocus for an annex while this business lasts. Can I cook anything? Can you think of anything I could fetch over ? "

" Aunty does everything. But if there should be, you shall. You are as good — Why, there 's a little bit of heaven in Ascutney Street, and I never knew it ! " Jane's voice filled up and broke while her face was bright with a smile. To come near to people, to find in them this hidden reality, behind all the little miserableness she had hated so, — it reproached her while it swelled her very heart with a gladness that was almost a sudden pain.

Mrs. Turnbull saw the pantomime of the scene from an upstairs window, — carefully kept closed,

— on what was, as she at this time had congratulated herself, the " blind side " of her own house.

" Rebecca Rickstack can't keep out of anything that's going on, not even diphtheria! I wonder when she went and got so intimate *there ;* and with Jane Gregory, too! Squeezing hands and all but kissing! *I do give up !* "

All she said aloud was the last sentence of four words, and that with intense deliberation ; the rest had rushed from her mental lips only, distinct, if not articulate. *What* she gave up was not clear to herself, perhaps ; it might even be, as with terrible prognostication, Ascutney Street itself and altogether.

Jane sent a note around by the tray and Aunty and the box-lift. Things were very much like " Through the Looking-Glass," she could not help reflecting in the midst of her anxieties.

In these days, she and Alice lived a good deal behind the looking-glass, in the clever story, and in the suggestions that arose from it. I may as well put in here — although to the interruption of what was immediately forthcoming from the sending of the note — and the looking-glass world was full of just such interruptions — an illustration of such demurs and interpretations, on the one side and the other, as took place not infrequently between the two.

Alice always called Jane " Queen."

" Queen," she said one morning, " how quick you are! You dress like a daisy. The wind blows, and the sun shines, and there you are, all ready, as if the morning put your clothes on for you. And you look so *new* every day! "

Jane laughed. " And you talk as a brook runs; you don't go round hunting for drops of water; they come from the sky and the hills, and you can't help it. But, Alice, that White Queen was very untidy! "

" I know she was; but that was the wrong-side-out part; that's the queerness of the looking-glass; you can't tell what everything meant. But she was so good and kind, the dear White Queen! She had nobody to 'ad-dress' but herself, you know; and everything was crooked."

That turned Jane silent. She thought all at once how untidy she had truly often let herself be, in that inside world where she was so alone, and things so crooked. She began to discover very keen applications in the funny parable.

" ' Jam yesterday, and jam to-morrow, and never any jam to-day; ' I think it was a hard way to live, for a queen," said the child, thoughtfully drawing on her stockings.

Jane came suddenly to her help, put her arms around her from behind, and clasped her close for an instant as she did so, burying quick, warm little kisses in the tangle of her curls.

" Why do you kiss me, Queen, in such a hurry ? "

" Because you 're in behind the looking-glass, and I 'm so glad of you; and nobody ever came before," said Jane.

When Miss Rickstack came over to the little orchard-place below the steps again, with a bunch of bright carnations in her hand to leave for Mrs. Sunderland and Jane, and two or three fastened in the white kerchief that was gathered about her own neck, Jane had to seize a little inward pang of jealousy as by the throat, and strangle it. It was quickly, resolutely done, though; and she gave Mrs. Sunderland's message of warm thanks, and took Alice's other hand to let her walk between them over to The Crocus.

" Why here I am between the Queens," cried Alice, with a hop-skip of delight. " Every bit of it is coming true. Only you don't push, and things won't be helter-skelter, and I sha'n't pull the table-cloth down, nor shake you into a kitten ! " Which was all Greek to Miss Rebecca Rickstack, who did not even know she was a Red Queen.

Jane left Alice ecstatically happy with wonderful things that had belonged to two generations, themselves two and three generations back from the present.

Miss Rickstack had, with reckless lavishness of resource, set them all out at once upon a big table; but their various capabilities would not be exhausted in many visits. There was a little fireplace of baked clay, with a chimney, a perfect model of the great-grandmothers' fireplaces before ranges and cookstoves were: crane and hooks and hangers, pots and kettles, and irons, tin-kitchen and tin-baker to set before the fire. There was a tiny cheese-press with wooden screws; an upright churn and dasher; a miniature spinning-wheel. Set apart from these were modernized appliances: a stove which would burn charcoal, with real covers, boiler, steamer, saucepans and frying-pan, and a cubby of an oven in the side that would bake a pie as big as a half dollar, or a loaf of bread two inches long. In another group, a complete little set of stuffed drawing-room furniture, green, with gold bands, a mirror and a bookcase, all of a real old-fashionedness not old enough to be revived in the craze of the new style, but absolutely forgotten. And there was store of tea-set and dinner-set china in piles of plates and cups and saucers; these, too, of varying patterns and periods, enough to set any little girl's heart in a whirlwind of delight.

"You shall make pats of butter, and pans of gingerbread for Rick, as fast as he gets better," said Miss Rickstack, and Alice hovered over and handled the pretty toys with a true little house-wife's lovingness and dainty touch.

"Now will you keep house fifty years ago, or twenty years ago, or to-day?" the Red Queen was asking as Jane turned away, to go back to duties she was set free for, and to watch and listen through the critical hours upon which so much was hanging.

As she came in at the little lower gate, she saw a stranger at the front door — a gentleman. He had just dropped the written card from his fingers and was laying hand upon the bell-knob.

"If you please, sir!" called Jane hurriedly, making her way toward the piazza end across the grass. The visitor turned and walked toward her, meeting her at the side steps. "I don't think" — and then she caught her breath. The two looked at each other.

"Doctor Hansell!" said the girl to herself; spelling the name mentally, as she always did, with two *l*'s.

"J. G.!" ejaculated Doctor Hans, also mentally, without any question of orthography, or fact.

There she stood, in what might have been the identical soft gray dress, a blue veil tied over the fawn-brown hair lying in the same little feathery locks upon the clear, sweet brow. And there was he, the same strong, upright, manly figure, lifting his hat to her as he had done that long-ago morning in the old Bay Line station-house; the same kindly, courteous look, dwelling, as it had done then, upon the face uplifted to him; a gleam of surprised recognition added, which she could well see, and to which her own eyes involuntarily answered.

Several confused ideas were flitting through the doctor's head. Could he have mistaken the house? This girl — J. G. — belonged here, evidently, — a strange coincidence! Question, relief, perplexity, fear, and pleasure, all had time in a single instant to complicate themselves in features capable of most swift and delicate differencing of expression.

Jane waited. She could not say now what she had begun, of refusal or inquiry. It was for Dr. Hansell to make his own demand. Beyond that involuntary glance, neither claimed anything. A graver matter had immediate precedence.

"Is this — I beg pardon — Mrs. Sunderland's house?" came the question.

"Yes. And you see there is sickness."

"I see. Severe? Who is it?" The words were of telegraphic brevity. The face was intent upon hers for the answer.

"Not desperate. Hopeful, I think. Little Rick." Jane replied, with as instant precision.

" Tell her I am here. Doctor" — he paused slightly, hesitating whether to be so abrupt.

"I know — Doctor Hansell," said Jane Gregory. "It will not hurt her. She will be glad. Will you wait here a moment? I do not go into the front of the house at all. I have charge of Alice. I will send some one."

With which concise explanation she left him in some unsuspected surprise, and took her swift way to the staircase entrance, and to communication from above with Aunty.

Then it all came to him as he stood there. The "White Queen" of Gretel's letter. This was she. That she should also be J. G., and why she should have called him Dr. Hansell, were points to be put aside and thought of later. A moment more, and he was in the house; a fleet step was on the stair; a voice, hushed, yet keen with joy, cried, "Hans! O Hans! This *is* God's sending! How? — But *that* was how!" And Margaret had her arms about his neck.

"I was in Chicago, and just ran on. Now let me come right up."

That night Rick was out of imminent danger; but Margaret had the sickness. "In time; only just in time," she said, with fresh thanksgiving, resigning Rick into his uncle's hands, and giving herself up to be cared for.

Dr. Griffith telegraphed to his comrade in Sunnywater, and stayed on in Ascutney Street.

CHAPTER IX

"How easy things happen when they once begin!" said Miss Rickstack, "and then, again, they
won't start for a lifetime."

"Just so," said Aunty. "When you're ready,
they come; when you're unready, they tarry, and
you all slumber and sleep. Who knows how much
sooner — But I won't take liberties with Scripcher.
All *I* want is to see a straight way, and happen-
in's likewise, as if they *was* sent, and did n't jest
tumble. Then I don't care which way, — least I
try not to. But there's a great many wee-waws,
hither-an'-yons, and criss-cross, till you can't see
what Providence itself is up to. And in your own
mind the worst; whether to do, or whether you've
done ; and thinking whether you've *done* is awful!"

Miss Rickstack and Aunty were great friends in
these days; but these days were a little further on.
There had been some hard "wee-waws" first. One
was the night when Margaret was at the worst, and
the nurse was worn out, and only Doctor Hansel
fit to watch either patient. "And he would n't be,
only he's a man," said Aunty, with touching confi-

¹ence in the strength of the stronger sex. She
ᵈd Jane still called the doctor by his fairy-tale
name, Aunty from habit, Jane from mistake, just
touched with a doubt that there was a mistake
somehow. When she could, without confusing
him with Dr. Escue, she used only the medical title.

"It's a wee-waw," Aunty said; "only it won't
swing clear e'er-a-way, more'n an inch."

Jane gave it a push. "We will leave Alice
over at The Crocus, and I'll go up," she said.
"We must do the best thing, and that is it."

"She can't come back again!" cried Aunty, in
amazement.

"Of course not. But I must take the responsibility now. She is perfectly safe and happy. Mrs.
Sunderland will approve when — she knows."
There was a sob in the break between the words,
but it was kept down with a brave face.

Aunty could not so well hold back the emotion
to which the contagion of Jane's gave release.
She sat down on the lower step of the garden stair,
whence she had held counsel with Jane at the top,
and put her face between her hands upon her
knees. "Don't speak to me!" she choked forth
with very poor disguise; "I'm — think — ing!"

Jane stepped back into the white room; a moment after, when she came forth again, Aunty was

on her feet, pouring from a broken-nosed pitcher some carbolized water upon the step where she had been sitting. "'T ain't *my* resk, either way," she was saying; "nor sha'n't be. Don't come down till I'm clear off," she called up hurriedly. "I might forget, if you was within arm's reach, you — dear, blessed, contrary creechur!"

That night, when the hush and dusk had settled upon the sick - rooms, — the night-lamps placed, the nurse gone to bed for a three hours' rest, and Rick in his first sleep, — Dr. Griffith, passing along the little corridor to his sister's room, saw the swing-door to the long L-passage gently slip ajar, and a white figure enter noiselessly from beyond. Jane Gregory met him, in soft, silent raiment, straight skirts and sacque-wrap of starchless cambric, fresh ones upon her arm to replace with, and a little linen bag in her hand. She stopped, just over the rubicon, when she saw him.

"You here! Miss" — began Dr. Hansell.

"Yes. I am Jane," the girl answered low. "I have come to stay with Rick. I knew somebody was needed."

"But — I don't know what to do with you!" The tone in which the doctor was obliged to speak was inadequate to express his half-annoyed, entirely perplexed astonishment.

"There is nothing for you to do," Jane answered,

"except to put up with me." In the dim light he saw that she smiled quietly. "I shall sit by Rick. The nurse can sleep, and you will have only Mrs. Sunderland." She moved forward to pass on.

"What have you done with Alice? You can't go back, you know."

"I know. She is at Miss Rickstack's. She can stay."

"The best place for her," said the doctor briefly. "You have left me nothing to object to — except — yourself. And now we must leave that where we leave everything we can't help. You are a brave woman, Jane."

She had given him nothing else to call her by but her little Christian name. He might have left that off; but that he did not sent a curious feeling through Jane's consciousness. It was as if he had taken her by the hand.

"If there are any particular directions" — she began, as she went by into the doorway of Rick's room, where she turned and paused. But the doctor came in also. He put something into a glass with water, and told her to drink it. Then he prepared another similar portion, which he covered and set upon the mantel. "Take that at twelve o'clock," he said. "Give Rick a teaspoonful of this upon the table every hour when awake. Offer him milk also. It is in the little cooler. Water

when he asks for it. I shall be in once or twice
before morning. Keep him as quiet as possible.
Sleep before everything." With these brief sentences, he went away.

He had treated Jane precisely as she chose to be
treated. He had understood, and had taken her
at her word. She felt received into confidence and
trust. More: she had entered into rapport with a
high, strong, sincere nature.

In the two adjoining rooms these two sat, anxious, intent upon their watch, yet singularly conscious of each other; wondering, each how the
other had again come in the way, and now so
closely.

In the morning, Mrs. Sunderland was easier;
the doctor came and treated Rick's throat, which
was nearly in its normal condition. Jane was not
tired; she knew how to take even watching with a
certain repose of nerve. The nurse had had full
rest, and resumed her post with Mrs. Sunderland;
Dr. Griffith went off for a nap; Jane stayed with
Rick, and told him little inexciting stories. The
child was happy. His mother did not know that
Jane was there.

Dr. Griffith managed to learn somehow the rest
of Jane's name; the next time he had occasion to
make use of it, he addressed her as Miss Gregory.
She was not a housemaid, nor a nursemaid; she

felt the delicate respect and courtesy; but she liked to remember that once saying of " Jane." For her part, she had found out no more concerning his; she had got used to thinking of him as Dr. Hansell, and she did not care; it was easy enough to call him "Doctor." Of course he was Mrs. Sunderland's near relative ; her brother, doubtless; but what Mrs. Sunderland's maiden name had been she did not know. It was pleasant — she did not ask herself why — still to think of him as Dr. Hansell. She was in no hurry to begin her acquaintance with him over again under a strange appellation ; " Dr. Hansell" held all her associations thus far.

She was considering far more another circumstance which, indeed, at this juncture did not matter much, but would trouble her honesty by and by. That she knew a little more of Mrs. Sunderland's brother than Mrs. Sunderland was aware of, — that she was keeping to herself the fact of that first meeting, — that recognition of herself in the doctor's little written story of it, — all this must be held account with by and by. She was very conscious that it had not been a light, forgotten matter with her; if it had been, it would not be presenting itself as a stern question of candor now. But these things waited.

What Dr. Griffith thought did not appear.

On the second day, all possible precautions taken, he had Jane and Rick transferred to the white room, where he watched over their well-being by open-air colloquies on the staircase, and by minute directions for Jane's proceeding and observation with the child and with herself.

Always quiet, always simple and direct, there was nothing in Jane's manner but earnest attention and entire occupation with the duties in hand. Sometimes, notwithstanding that first electric look that he knew had shot between them, he very nearly doubted if she positively remembered. But he, no more than she, passed, by any word or sign, the limits which the present time imposed.

For the by-and-by a question waited with the doctor also, which was fast taking shape as a determination. He had time to arrange his tactics clearly in his own mind; that was where he had advantage of the girl. She would have to be taken by surprise whenever and however he might make allusion or inquiry.

It came the day before Mrs. Sunderland was to go downstairs again. There was no more time to lose.

The doctor met Jane as she took her little constitutional among the apple-trees. Dr. Escue had just left, his visits ended with this one; things were glad and bright in the little house now; they were going to be very busy. Final fumigating and cleansing, — one part at a time; then packing and moving, for a change was prescribed and imperative. Whither, Jane did not know, nor how far it would concern herself; she had a talent for not asking questions.

" Good-morning, Miss Gregory."

" Good-morning, Doctor."

" You have not got farther all this time than the handle to my name. I have never been properly presented. Yours had n't one, — suitably available, — so I was obliged to inform myself. Dr. Griffith, at your command, Miss Gregory." And the doctor lifted his hat and bowed.

Jane laughed gently, frankly; at the same time she too bent her head. "Thank you," she replied.

"Do you mind telling me," said Dr. Griffith, with something of a quiet, professional method of steadily working to a point, " how you happened at first to call me Dr. Hansell ? "

" Did you notice that ? " asked Jane, a little disturbed. " I — The children called you so, Dr. Griffith."

" Yes. Before you saw me, — before I came, I mean. How, please, did you identify me ? "

This was a bad corner; from which Jane came straight out.

" If you please, Dr. Griffith, I would rather not

tell you that. I cannot quite explain it now." It was said with the shyest deference, and yet with a sweet courage of directness, her eyes raised confidently to the courtesy in his.

Dr. Griffith bowed again. He treated her as if she were a princess, this rare, high-mannered gentleman.

"I think you are a very spirit of truth," he said. "And truth has it all her own way. The eternal years are hers. I will wait." He smiled. And then he began to tell her what he and his sister had decided.

"We are all to go away," he said. "A little salt-air tonic, an out-of-door life awhile in this beautiful weather, is what you must all have." As if Jane were really one of them!

"There is a little place down among the rags and fringes of the Maine coast that we know, — that my brother-in-law leased one summer, and that we can have again, — Leeport Island; only three houses on it. Cliffs, and sea, and beach, and woods, all in a strip of a mile's length by a half mile in width at the broadest. Shall you like it?"

Again that making her of importance; that counting her in, not merely by permission, but as a motive. She was to be thought of, also; cared for. Jane's eyes shone with more than pleasure.

"You are *good*," she said with her simple emphasis.

Dr. Griffith answered nothing to that; he very slightly raised his hat again and went away.

There was nothing in the colloquy to neighboring eyes, — and the eyes were not wanting, — beyond the highly interesting and suggestive daily movements about the isolated and guarded house. What this, that, and the other meant in the proceedings and precautions casually apparent was a wonderfully sustaining object in life just now to Mrs. Turnbull, interrupted, as she was, in the ordinary autumn absorption of wardrobe readjustment. The "blind side" of her dwelling was vantage-ground for keenest observation.

In a few days, Jane came as far as the fence, and opened parley. The washerwoman was hanging linens upon the line, and with message by her Mrs. Turnbull was summoned.

She came cautiously as far as the larch-tree.

"Everything has been scalded and fumigated, and we are all well again. You need not be at all afraid," said Jane. "But I thought I would not come until you knew."

"Oh, I'm not afraid; but then it's always well enough to be careful. It's been a pretty serious thing in the neighborhood, this sickness."

"*In* the neighborhood, — yes," said Jane; "*for*

the neighborhood, there has been no danger. Everybody has been careful."

"Everybody except Rebecca Rickstack," Mrs.
Turnbull replied, accepting the commendation. "I
really think the Board of Health ought to have
interfered with her. Back and forth, trailing mi-
crobes up and down the sidewalk! Is the little
girl there now?"

"She sleeps and eats there. She came to see
her mother yesterday."

"And you've been in the end room, have n't
you? Taking your meals in from the stairs?
And who was that you talked to, on the steps, and
in the garden?"

"Aunty?" asked Jane naughtily.

"Aunty! As if I did n't know *her!* The
man."

"That was the doctor."

"Not Dr. Escue?"

"No. The other one. He stayed all the time,
after the worst began."

Dr. Griffith had betaken himself to the city for
lodgings since the recoveries were certain. True
as she was, Jane did not feel obliged to explain
everything to Mrs. Turnbull.

"He's a mighty polite man. Lives mostly with
his hat in his hand, I should think. What's his
name?"

"He is always polite," remarked Jane, in acquiescence. "They have ordered us off," she made haste to say, and to transfer Mrs. Turnbull's solicitudes to her own affairs. "And that is my errand now. I hope you won't think I've deserted you, but maybe you'd as lief have me after I have been away among the sea breezes."

"That's it, is it? Well, I can get along somehow; I suppose I must. What's Miss Rickstack going to do to get aired off? I don't think she need put out her red ribbons yet awhile, anyway. Ascutney Street folks won't trouble her much at present."

"Miss Rickstack is to go with us," said Jane.

"*Where?*" demanded Mrs. Turnbull, staring. Jane stated briefly.

A little bell tinkled from the white room window, and she turned to go.

"Well, I *do* give up," came after her, in solemn intonation.

But Mrs. Turnbull did not give up. She was never farther from it. She struggled with the surprise and problem all day. When Mr. Turnbull came home, she presented the subject to him, in her habitual inverted fashion.

"I never thought Rebecca Louisa Rickstack was quite a fool, before," she observed, handing her husband his second cup of tea. "It is certainly a most astonishing thing."

" That a woman should be a fool? or that you should find a fool out? "

" I don't see how she can ever have the face to come into Ascutney Street again! "

" Perhaps she 'll back in. It is an impressive way to do anything."

" I don't know what you mean," said Mrs. Turnbull, aware that her husband was chaffing her as usual, but missing the point.

" There we are in perfect sympathy, my dear. Did n't you forget the sugar in this tea? "

" She 's going off with those Sunderlands — and Jane Gregory — to some little down-east place that they came from," said Mrs. Turnbull, pouring out her news and a ladleful of sugar, at one dash, into Mr. Turnbull's ears and his extended cup. Mr. Turnbull drew back with what he had received, and tasted his amended beverage — and intelligence — in silence.

" Folks might have got over what she did, off-hand, in time of sickness, if it had stopped there. But this is in cold blood."

" Diabolical. I mean the tea. But no matter."

" You 're a very funny man," said his wife, with severe irony. " Everybody thinks so. But everybody does n't know what it is to have to live all the time with a funny man, and tell him things in earnest."

" Perhaps if you could be just a little less in earnest, — it 's hard for a person sensitive to impressions to stand too much, you know," and Mr. Turnbull sipped ruefully his over-sweetened tea. " But 'telling things in earnest' is good. I like that. It 's apt to be a woman's way; and a man has to be funny, or otherwise."

" Wait till you hear what Mrs. Inching will say," answered his wife undivertedly.

" I 'm not obliged to hear that; I 'm not Mr. Inching." He left the table, and lighted his cigar. A woman has no such refuge. It would not have been a refuge for a woman like Mrs. Turnbull. She could not so have broken off an argument.

CHAPTER X

Two things Dr. Griffith had said to Jane Greg-ory, which would have remained her possession, though he should never have spoken to her again. He had said that she was a brave woman; he had called her a very spirit of truth. But it began to be a trouble in her mind, the doubt whether she were continuing either.

Several times, now, she had sat alone with Mrs. Sunderland, when there had been opportunity, so far as that went, to have explained to her the one fact which she felt the latter had a right to know. But the declaration assumed so much in the very making, that it interposed an impossibility. How was she, an unpretending earner of her bread, — now, indeed, in Mrs. Sunderland's own employ, — to presume to make it of consequence that she had met the lady's brother, Dr. Griffith, two years before; that he had then rendered her a trifling inci-dental service, and that she had remembered it and him ever since? That she had understood, and taken to herself, all that he had said in that letter; that she had known him the moment she had

met him; and that she had ke ᵀ
now?

Every day made it harder. And yet Mₐ
derland ought to know. To continue to holu
back, Jane felt, was to make it increasingly significant. Significant to herself. Jane was conscious
of that reality, and did not mean to suffer it. If,
indeed, Dr. Griffith had forgotten — but she was
well aware that he had not. It must be done ; and
yet she must do it with as little show and forcing
of purpose as might be. So it was but just before
the flitting from Ascutney Street that time and
way came to her.

She was helping Mrs. Sunderland pack a large
box that was to go to Bay Hill. Jane knew about
Bay Hill, now ; at the end of its summer lease
Mrs. Sunderland would return there for the pres-
ent; Dr. Griffith had persuaded her. Ascutney
Street was to be given up.

The two sat together, quietly busy, folding and
placing. The children were at Miss Rickstack's ;
Dr. Griffith was in town.

" I should never have undertaken this but for
my brother," Margaret said, a little wearily. " It
is so good of him to stay and see us settled. But
I know it will do him good also. He cannot live
altogether without sea air. He is barely amphib-
ious as to climate, and will always have to come

east of the Alleghanies to store up native atmosphere, he says.   And just now there is a young
medical man out near Sunnywater, to whom he has
lent a start, as he calls it.   He manages to make
the wind blow both ways, — ill to nobody."

"I think Dr. Griffith is always good," said Jane
calmly.   But her head was pretty well over in the
packing-box.   When she lifted it up, and sat facing Mrs. Sunderland, her hands for a moment lay
quietly upon her lap, while her friend hesitated between certain next parcels.   She would not say
her next words under cover, as if she needed any.

"It was Dr. Griffith — I was the girl, I mean,
whose hat blew off upon the train, once, and he
got it for her.   There were a hundred people there,
but only one Dr. Griffith."

Then she took the package in order and put it
down into the box, directly to the best place, fitting
it in with perfect care and attention.   She turned
to receive another, with the same honest self-com-
mand, although the silence of a half moment in
which she did so seemed long to her.   Of what was
Mrs. Sunderland thinking?

"Then you recognized the details of that little
story for Alice — in the letter?"   In the slowness
with which the question came, and was uttered,
Jane perceived precisely what she had expected:
that another question lay behind, which she knew

Mrs. Sunderland would not like to put to her downrightly, — "Why did you not tell me then?"

"I recognized the things that happened, — and Dr. Griffith," Jane replied, without embarrassment. "He made it rather hard for me to recognize myself."

"What a good packer you are, Jane!" said Mrs. Sunderland.

Jane looked a little surprised at the sudden turn; but it was no turn at all. Mrs. Sunderland only applied to Jane's sentences an illustration from her obvious work. Everything had been gotten into them. Every fact that it was her own right to know was there, at her service, but in as little extension as possible. Care had been taken to present the whole truth; but conclusions had been left to take care of themselves. There was no secret now, in Jane's memory, concerning Dr. Griffith; she made no secret of her own appreciation of him; she explained, without explaining, how impossible it must have been for her, at the moment, to claim all that the story in the letter said of the girl about whom it was told. The rest she left to Mrs. Sunderland, with that reposefulness of an entire unconcealment which was mere relief to Jane, but which Mrs. Sunderland was more than half uncertain whether to set down to personal unconcern or not. She felt almost rebuked by Jane's pure

directness for the slight obliquity, the little ten-
tativeness, that had been in her own first leading
observation.

For Dr. Griffith had already told his sister all
that Jane had now, to Mrs. Sunderland's better
satisfaction, volunteered. Soon after her convalescence had begun, he had acquainted her with the
circumstances — very "like a story," Margaret
said — which had brought him first to Chicago,
and thence home.

A young fellow, who had been in Colorado for
the benefit of his health, had been very ill at Den-
ver, and when as far on his way back as Sunnywater had suffered a dangerous relapse. Dr. Griffith had attended him; had found that, though he
could help him to such a degree of convalescence
as might make it possible for him to reach home, it
would be a painful, hazardous journey, and there
was no ultimate hope. The boy, who was but
twenty, and had conceived the clinging attachment
to the doctor which his character and service in
such loneliness and need had naturally drawn
forth, begged him to see him safe through. "My
father will make it as right as he can," he had
said; and the expression which simply meant the
inadequacy of money to make it even at all, Dr.
Griffith had put aside as significant of some partial limit in the means; and for that very rea-

son, white knight as he was, had left the Sunny-water business to the hands of his associate, had taken the youth to his father, and had watched with the old man by the death-bed which proved, as he had feared, the goal of the journey.

To his astonishment, the old gentleman handed him on his departure, not only a check which was ample remuneration for medical services and time, but papers which transferred to him the value of ten thousand dollars, " at the request of his boy," he said, " whose separate bit of property it was by a legacy, and which he could not, as a minor, bequeath by will. Take it," the old man had said to his remonstrance. " I am solitary now, and I have two hundred times as much that must go somewhere to help strangers ; and you are no stranger."

So Dr. Griffith had come on east for his holiday, and storage of Atlantic atmosphere, having telegraphed to his friend, " Shall be away a week or two longer. Hold on at Sunnywater for good."

" I was glad," he said, " to be able to settle that. I 've taken a fancy to him ; he 's a kind of Tom Thurnall, — a born naturalist and chemist ; just the fellow to take in a big prairie range, and be everywhere at once. And it has made this easy for me, all through ; though I should have stayed, anyway, finding you as I did. Your case took precedence of all else."

"And now?" Margaret had asked; the two words including a great deal, both as to movement and motive, but throwing the burden upon him of understanding and answer.

"I have not quite done with you; and my own case still remains," he replied.

She could gather very little from this, but she felt instinctively that something was to be gathered, beyond the fact that he had, as yet, secured not much to himself of the fine climatic reinforcement he had come for.

When, however, in the course of more varied talk afterward, they spoke of Jane Gregory, and to his straightforward commendation of her, "Not a failure in her; not a pretense about her!" he added quietly, "I knew that was the sort of woman she was, Margaret, the first time I ever saw her," Margaret naturally looked up at him with a wondering question coupled with her eager interest.

"The first time was on that train in from Exham, at the Wing Street station," Dr. Griffith said, "when her hat blew off, and I telegraphed back for it, — I wrote you the little incident. It was queer to meet her here again in the midst of this."

It had been spoken with the simplest composure, and, as Jane did now, he had left the fact with

Margaret for such induction as she pleased, changing the subject to other matters.

But John Griffith rarely spoke mere casual words.

How like these two were to each other in the force of their plain reality! To what might this force swiftly tend? And in other things so different; was it well?

Yet what were the "other things," after all? Margaret was driven to ask herself this, in her own sincerity. Were they things, or shadows, — the "vain show" in which people walk, disquietedly, or the verities which the shows simulate? Upon the plane of these verities did not the differences vanish?

She determined to put it all aside, into the future which should be responsible for itself. There was nothing else for her to do. A bit of wisdom from the looking-glass story flashed up in her mind. The queen had not pricked her finger yet; if she cried or worried about that, she would be living backward.

There was something laid off from each individual mind of the party, as they set forward on their pleasant seaward journey. A certain sense of freedom and fresh permission, of all being fair and understood, which nobody stopped to analyze, pervaded their relations. They had furlough for a happy holiday.

The children effervesced; Miss Rickstack beamed and glowed continually. She had never had so large, so sweet a slice of life before.

" Mamma," said Rick, leaning up by his mother's side as they sat upon the deck of the little Bath steamer, gliding down into the breadths and water-glades and islanded beauty of the great river *débouchure,* — " Mamma, what a big, beautiful world! It was awful little in Ascutney Street ! "

" Maybe you did n't know the whole of it. It was big enough to hold those two," and Mrs. Sunderland gave a bright, warm look over toward Jane and Miss Rickstack, who had placed themselves slightly aside. They often chose to pair off so, and leave a little family seclusion possible. Aunty sat in the middle of a stack of handbags, shawl-straps, and umbrellas. The share she took to herself was to " keep counted up."

" Mamma," said Alice, " it did n't hold them. They were on the wrong side of the looking-glass, where everything is queer ; and they came through to us. Jane says she is n't the White Queen, though ; she 's nothing but a little pawn on our chessboard. Mamma Margaret, I 've been thinking it all out. I think there 's a whole row of looking-glass houses, one after another, just as there was at Bay Hill, you know, where they were opposite, in the buff parlor, and you could see on

and on, till you couldn't see anything. I think
it's make-believe one side, and come-true the
other; and we are in the looking-glass of the next
one till we get in there, and then we're looking-
glass to the next, and we grow realer and realer
every time, till we get away in — to heaven!"

"And a chessboard game in every one?" asked
Uncle Hans.

"I suppose so," said Alice, gravely.

"It seems to me I remember that things were a
good deal upset in Looking-glass House, — queens
and kings and castles down among the ashes,
crowding up close to the chimney in a hurry to get
through; and that somebody said, 'Mind the vol-
cano! don't get blown up; climb slowly, the regular way, and help yourself!'"

"They'd got off the board," said Alice. "The
only way is to go by the squares."

Uncle Hans and Mamma Margaret laughed out.

"But the knights and the queens have a good
deal to do with it, — helping people across, I
mean," said Alice.

The afternoon light was glowing low, and lovely.
They were winding in and out through straits and
cuts and rounding points; and beautiful shores
ran their green lines in curves and headlands, and
little clumps of woodland, or bare, soft pasture,
or gray rock, lifting up from the water, spotted

the wider expanses; and they never knew, looking forward, which way the boat would take as it threaded its course along, always down and down toward the open ocean.

By-and-by, when the sunshine streamed almost level, and the eastern slopes and edges were shining in a yellow glow, and the western ones taking deeper and deeper shadows, and the water turning gray or purple or black or golden as the gloom crept or the glory flashed, — in the midst of a fairy archipelago of small islets and a winding network of rippling river-paths between, they slowed and slipped up to a little pier, a rope was thrown around a mooring-post, a gang-plank flung across from deck to platform, and our party landed upon Leeport.

There was a cart to take their luggage, and an open one-horse wagon for those who needed to ride. Mrs. Sunderland and the children were bestowed in the vehicle; the others went forward on foot.

The soft, brown country road, plunging into green woods directly from the rocky river-face, took them into a sweet stillness and fragrance. Odors of pine and bay were accentuated—as color is in seaside blossoms — by the keen, soft tingle of the sea; the indescribable island atmosphere wrapped and penetrated them with exhilarating delight; the hush was softly touched with rhythmic sound by the rote upon a long ledge-beach some half mile or so away ; it seemed as if the drift of every day had borné them to a wonderful out-of-the-world quiet and blessedness, had swept them gently upon its shore, and gone fussing and struggling on, with puff and paddle, leaving them in a great release and peace.

It was the beginning of an idyl of days.

When Jane Gregory and Rebecca Rickstack thought of Ascutney Street, they marveled how Ascutney Street had ever got built upon an earth whose beginnings were like this ; how, being built, and they imprisoned in it, it had ever disappeared from them, and left them in this primal beauty. It was as if city, and tumult, and work, and crowd, and worry had melted away from them, and disembodied them of the world, leaving them to the very soul of things, unhampered and unspoiled.

It seemed queer, almost, to take their clothes out of their trunks, which they had packed according to their outer needs that pressed so close and so continually upon them in their old life ; "things" were a strange link between that far-away past and place and this.

Three houses on the island, as Dr. Griffith had told Jane. One was the little lighthouse, the first beacon on the inland channel, at the end of the long cliff ; another was the Morse farmhouse, a th substantial, well-to-do congeries of dwelling and outbuildings back upon the central upland; the third, this, — also a part of the Morse family property, whose former occupant had "taken the fever, and gone West," — down where the shore turned southerly, at the head of a beautiful little cove and soft-lapped beach. "Round the island," walk or drive, as the visitor chose to make it, wound the narrow wagon-track and side-path over brown earth and pine needles, in woody shades and by open shore, with breaks of cliff and ledge-crossings; now burying the passer in sweet, hidden solitudes, now carrying him close to the blue surge of water that kissed the sand, or tossed gay breakers up the spines of rocks; and again lifting him to a summit whence the great sweep of ocean one way, and the green slopes of the farm fields the other, could be overseen.

A path, which led from the old Morse house to the south cove, crossing the little side orchard of the cove house, and touching at its kitchen entrance with demonstration of family use and history, ran down to the small gravelly beach, sheltered on either hand by the high out-thrusts of the long ridge, against the base of which the cove cottage stood.

Southwesterly the ridge projected itself, narrowing and sharpening and rising higher; the driveway crept along behind it, as behind a rampart; on its crests were only bleak rock, mossy pasture grass, and hardy furze.

Down in the safe little cove, Rick and Alice played. Jane and Miss Rickstack sat with them, or found nooks above in cool, rocky niches, where they could watch the children and chat pleasantly together. In the afternoons, when it was loveliest, Dr. Griffith and Margaret would come out, with work or drawing, and books; and there would be reading and talk that were worth coming away into this distant security for; that could only so have been attempted and enjoyed.

It was the third morning after their arrival. Mrs. Sunderland was resting in her hammock, slung between two maple-trees in the front door-yard; Dr. Griffith had taken the morning boat up to Bath; and the others were in the rocky cove.

The children were sailing boats in the edge of the water, keeping them within control by tow-ing-lines of twine, the reflex wave carrying them out to full length from shore, and the next incom-ing one bringing them back with gentle slide upon the sand.

These boats were very childish and womanish af-fairs, such as Jane and Miss Rickstack could help make, with bits of shingle, and masts of wooden-skewer style, whittled from pine sticks. A sail of

curiously un-nautical fashion, with stays and hal-
yards arranged more with an amateur eye to effect
than with any technical knowledge, served as a
label to each one at least, that might say, " This is
intended for a vessel, and as such is to be politely
regarded."

They floated, however, and kept right side up
better than might have been expected ; their raft-
like proportion and the low, crosswise set of the
canvas, — for it was a bold adaptation of square-
rig to a sloop, — perhaps helping to this ; and the
young ones, knowing nothing better, and all unwit-
ting of certain memoranda in Uncle Hansel's
pocket-book among the errands which had taken
him to Bath, were satisfied ; while the elders were
divided between tender compunctions for the im-
position upon innocent confidingness and fun over
their own half-comprehended blunders.

A new craft was just launched, — the Jabberwock, whose name was stitched in red worsted letters upon the rectangle of cotton cloth, with osten-
tatious blazonry ; and a long, retreating lapse of
the outgoing tide was taking it finely forth, when a
sudden cry from Rick brought Jane hastily to his
aid, to find the frail hawser escaped from his small
fingers, and the Jabberwock galumphing off to sea
in earnest.

Jane had in her pocket her ball of twine from

which rigging and cables were made ; she unwound a goodly length of it, and fastened it to a branch of brushwood.

"Stand back, Rick," she said; "I'll try for it when the next wave comes in."

It had bobbed back and forth two or three times already, and the outward current was evidently getting the better ; but Jane stepped close to the edge of the water, and held the grapple ready for a fling.

They were all eagerly intent upon the effort, and nobody saw a small rowboat that had slipped suddenly through a narrow cut in the outreach of the ledge, in a deep, overhanging shadow, until a voice startlingly near called out, " Don't wet your feet, young lady ; I'll tow in the catamaran ! " and looking round, they saw the skiff shoot smoothly by, the oar just dropped in its bottom, the last spurt sending it straight in toward where they stood.

A young man with handsome sea-browned face and athletic figure, in blue woolen shirt, sat upon the middle thwart, and reaching out his arm in passing, caught, not the truant vessel itself in ignominious grasp, as he might have done, but with all respect the floating cable, by which, an instant after, as he sprang upon the beach, and dragged his own boat with one hand upon the gravel, he restored it to its owners.

Rick caught the line, while Jane stood back.

"Thank you, sir. Who are you? And what's a — what you called my ship?"

The young fellow laughed. "You're welcome," he said. "A catamaran is a flat vessel with one big sail, or none at all. Only it's generally made of three logs, instead of one board. But that does n't matter. And I'm Matt Morse."

Rick looked pleased and puzzled. "But you're not this — you're not *our* Mr. Morse!"

"I'm *this* Mr. Morse, anyway," was the reply. "Not Leeport, though; Morse's Neck. We're half of us Morses round this bit of water. Mr. Azel Morse is my uncle."

He smiled, and touched his cap as he spoke, directing his explanation chiefly, and his courtesy wholly, toward Jane.

"I've come round from Riggsville, with the mail for the house. Will you look it over, or shall I carry it right up?"

"Thank you," Jane said simply. "There can't be anything for me; so, if you are going, they will be much obliged."

He had time only for one more swift look, — which took in quite as much as the stare that would have been unpardonable, — and with another touch of his fingers to his cap, turned and sprang up the rough bank, over which he quickly disappeared from those below.

It was the first, but not the last, of Mr. Matthew Morse.

Rick's head was up; he came beside Jane proudly. "I like him," he said. "He knows a cat-or-a-man!"

CHAPTER XI.

THERE is not much risk in saying that there was at least no handsomer or better-liked young fellow, at that time, between Bath and Boothbay, than Mr. Matthew Morse. He was known all up and down the river.

The Morses were an old Kennebec County family, and had owned among them, first and last, enough island and other property to have made a small township. They were plain people, and the present representatives held to primitive ways of occupation and living.

Matthew's father, old Captain Zenas, was retired now upon his little peninsular farm. Matthew helped him, in odd ways and times, but had his own independent craft. He was a boatman from beginning to end of all that a boat needs or is good for. He had served an apprenticeship in a building-yard at Bath, and knew how to put a boat together from keel to gunnel, from deck to spindle. And wherever any sort of a boat could go, up and down the river-aisles and cuts and intricate channels, or along these torn and jagged Atlantic shores, Matthew Morse could take her. He built rowboats and dories, and sold them for the pleasure or use of holiday comers or busy residents; he had a trim little yacht of his own construction, in which he carried pleasure parties up and down along shore, to and from Squirrel and Mouse, and the other frequented summer resorts, around Bald Head to Harpswell, out to Damariscove and around Monhegan, up to Wiscasset, or even to Penobscot Bay and Castine.

In the winter, he did house carpentering, made and mended; he hauled in wood; he helped to house ice, feeding the elevator, sliding it over the long trams into the great storage buildings, whence the companies contract to take supplies. He also read and studied, building up, as well as he could, upon the foundation of a fair New England school education; and he reveled in stories of a great outside world — as he thought it — that he would go forth into some time, not realizing how outside and free he was, just here and already, himself.

While old Captain Zenas lived, his place was at home. Afterward — but he was too good a son to dwell much upon that afterward.

Beside employment, he had amusement; trust Matthew Morse for that. He was wanted at every gathering where sledge or skates could carry him, or anybody else; and, by his energy and social

indefatigability, fairly held together as a neighborhood a population scattered here and there over a
fifteen-mile area of snow and ice. There was nothing, apparently, that Matt Morse could not accomplish; the only point to find fault with was his own
absolute persuasion of the fact. He was master
of all the little world he knew; perhaps it was
time, in the order of his training as a human being,
that he should be shown another. A more difficult
one would do him good; would rouse into evidence
some greater but, as yet, dormant elements of his
nature.

When Matthew Morse first saw Jane Gregory,
that further world rolled open suddenly before
him.

Not that he knew or feared its inaccessibility.
He saw it, as the prince in the fairy tale saw the
enchanted island through the clear, invisible wall
of adamant. It looked beautiful and strange to
him; there was something in its aspect, different
he knew not how, but with a wonderful charm,
from what he had ever met before.

A composure that did not answer, in the fashion
of ordinary girlhood, to that first quick noting in
a man's admiring look, — or his look that had fair
cause and chance to be admiring, — that did not
meet with any shyest challenge, or demurest readi-
ness, or most covert curiosity the masculine scrutiny

and gauge, but was simply and exactly what it had been the moment before, and would be the moment after, — this showed in Jane Gregory, and surprised him, with a certain sense of new conditions to be met, a higher order of companionship to be won.

If it was not love at first sight with Matthew Morse, it was stimulation to see more, a sudden fascination of the possible.

Two things he learned within the half hour of their meeting, which gave him the courage of an open opportunity.

She had said, "There can't be anything for me," when he had offered her the looking over of the mail; and no girl would have said that who had the keen personal interest anywhere which is always expectation. He had asked questions of aunt Kreeshy, and had found out that she was not really of the city family, but just invited with them, — a "kind of friendly help," aunt Kreeshy guessed. So she was not one of the unreachable maidens of mirage with whose flitting summer presence came those perilous visions in mountain and sea mists, bewildering reflections of a life whose reality is far away beyond a safe, prohibited horizon.

It was growing late in the season; he had but few positive engagements on hand; he resolved that after this week, which he hoped would end them, he would make no more unless at Leeport. Aunt Kreeshy would be sure to want him. When she had boarders, or the uncle Lishe house was let, she always had plenty of plans for her visitors, if they did not make them for themselves.

He went in and out, with his free, careless grace, among them; he got readily into talk with Dr. Griffith; that gentleman soon found out what he could do for them, and secured him and his yacht for two or three sailing excursions that should only wait their own convenient day. "After this week," Matthew said, "there would be nothing else."

"He is a handsome creature," Margaret said, as he swung off one morning with easy stride, and disappeared with rapid springs down the broken rocks into the cove.

"A fine physique," said Dr. Griffith; "and a fine nature otherwise, I think, if it were all developed. Remarkable, anyway, in his present place and occupation. He leaves a certain spectrum of bright impression when he vanishes. You don't often see just such coloring."

It was true; eyes the hue of a new, ripe hazelnut, but with a flash and sparkle like light on a brown rippling brook; hair sun-bronzed and tawny-tipped, tossed back from a clear, square forehead, that showed fair-skinned where the hat had

shaded it; cheeks and throat ruddy like the warm
side of a dusky, mellow pear; even, white teeth
that made his smile splendid; and a way of catching and transmitting a gleam and shine of continual cheer and pleasure, that left its trail upon the
sense, as Dr. Griffith said, when he was gone; one
would say he could but make his welcome where
he came, and add zest to any playday party.

But somehow Jane Gregory felt that he was going to interrupt them all. She thought she liked
the still times best.

It was beautiful in those days before the yacht-
ing was to begin.

Miss Rickstack was afraid of a rowboat, and she
was absolutely happy with the children; so Margaret and her brother took Jane with them on delicious little cruises, when they seemed to lose
themselves in pleasant bends and channels, and to
penetrate into myst rious windings and distances
of the water world. Whole afternoons they spent
thus upon the river, finding out new pictures and
pretty nooks; landing often in still places where
they could fancy no one had ever set foot before;
gathering wild vines of glossy leafage that crept
about the woodland soil, or filling tiny baskets with
the red partridge berries for Rick and Alice, and
making addition to their housekeeping array in
acorn cups of chosen size and beauty. Some of

these Mrs. Sunderland painted with minutest daintiness, like fairy decoration, with buds and bells of little, lowly, hiding things that bloom almost invisible, with tips of crimson mosses, or smallest fern-fringes.

Miss Rickstack had packed a fair-sized trunk, less with her own wardrobe than with surprises for the children, in the toys of olden time that Alice had lamented leaving; and the pats of butter and the little loaves of cake were forthcoming almost daily now in rivalry of aunt Kreeshy's bountiful supplies.

One evening they had gone up and around Button Island, a green knoll alone in the midst of a wide open, where sometimes a tired yoke of oxen was turned to pasture after a heavy season of summer work.

They had climbed to the highest point of rock, and sat there in the falling dusk, watching the first stars come out over the water, and the distant south light flash its safety-fire across the far-down strait. They could hear the antiphon of three sand beaches, calling to each other through the coming night, as the surf curled crisply up their sides and, shattering itself softly, fell back with a long whisper to the sea. And then they had rowed home in the early darkness, the phosphorescent water parting in sparkles under their bow, and dripping like pale electric fire from each lift of the oars.

Dr. Griffith knew the shore-marks and the way; he never undertook anything he was not prepared for. It was a delight to trust to such sure guidance, and the kindly care with which he watched and arranged their comfort was such a thing to share in! It was this sharing that made the charm for Jane. It was such privilege, and yet could be so meekly, simply taken.

They did not talk a great deal; the intercourse was but the deeper for the silence; and when there was speech it was of something, like the night and the light and the waters, to be remembered and dwelt in when the time itself had passed.

"How grand and sweet the wilderness is!" said Margaret, as they drifted down the strong current, where oars were not needed, under the overhanging walls of a deep cut, fringed and draperied from water edge to summit, with beautiful wood growths. They could only see them as a cloud, in the dimness, but the breath of them mingled with the clean water smell, and the stirs of boughs in the wind helped out the music of the breaking ripples.

"I wonder if the Wilderness of the Fasting was not some such place, and not a great, bare, burned-out desert of hunger and thirst. I wonder if He had not forgotten to be bodily hungry and thirsty, where everything was so full of the word He said men live by ! "

"He went there to be tempted, — it says," said Jane, with gentle doubt wistful to be dispelled.

"He went for what awaited him — as we all go; as He went up afterward to Jerusalem," said Dr. Grffith. "And both times, you see, He went *up*, and with a prelude of rejoicing. It is in the highest, sweetest places of our nature that we are tempted, and that we suffer."

"Always ? " asked Jane. "I thought it was so often in the mean and low."

"The mean and low are the degradations. It is only the high that can be profaned. It is the glory of the human that it is tempted."

"But vice is positive," said Margaret. "It is not always virtue perverted, or in disguise. Witness drunkenness, and all brutality."

"Ah, but which way do they witness? Of some things in themselves great and beautiful, — exaltations, affections, — whose inversions only the possible celestial can mistake for its very good. Satan is a fallen angel."

They came out into the dawning light of a far rising moon. Neither spoke again, until Margaret said, a little lightly, as if the thought and silence were oppressive, —

"Looking-glass inversions, Hans; that is like what you mean, I think. How much we have found out in that nonsense story!"

"Because it is n't nonsense," answered John. "I begin to doubt if anything ever is."

"That reminds me," spoke Jane suddenly. "Rick said such a queer wise thing one day to Alice, Mrs. Sunderland. It was after you had put away some book that you thought silly. 'Alice,' he said, 'I can tell you one thing. There is n't a single — bit — of trash — in the Bible!'"

"A very good postulate to start from," said Rick's uncle, laughing. "When we have got at a little of the truth in everything, we shall be saved a great many of our troublesome arguments about the authenticities of Scripture."

"I have heard people talk of it as trash, if they did n't call it so," said Jane.

"It is a book which answers to what a man brings to it, as his own face answers to him in the water," said Dr. Griffith.

"Is that all? Must we bring all that we are to find?"

The query came disappointedly.

"The answer is larger than the question, or it is no answer at all. And as to bringing, — who knows, but for the answering, what he does bring? A man's face is the thing in all the world that he cannot see directly," said Dr. Griffith.

Jane thought how good it was to bring askings to such counsel.

"Thank you," she said gently, as one who had received a gift. If she had known how glad Dr. Griffith was that he could give to her!

CHAPTER XII

" I AM going to take Miss Gregory off for a long walk," said Dr. Griffith, one morning later, " as a prescription. She sits about too much with the children. Don't disclaim; I know you like it; but I want you to take something, for your good, whether you like it or not."

" I am taking everything for my good, just now, I think," said Jane, and her quiet face glowed.

Margaret Sunderland wished for a moment, in one of her accesses of responsibility, that she were sure of that. She wished she were as sure as usual of Dr. John's infallibility.

As the two went across the field path together, they met Matt Morse coming to the house. He had in his hand a cluster of late wild things; the strawberry leaves of dark green enamel that grow low in the wet wood-edges; the tip of a maple branch that was set among them like a red rose spray; a single tender feather of the princess pine standing up beside it; a bit of trailing, delicate-leaved vine looped round and dropping over all.

He held it out to Jane. "There isn't very

much now," he said ; " but what there is, is
pretty."

" You are very kind," said Jane, and took it ;
but she did not say " I thank you," with the sweet
clearness of deliberate meaning that Dr. Griffith
knew.

A glimpse at her side face showed the doctor
that she blushed, and that a constrained hesitation
was upon her. What ailed her ordinary frankness ? Something in Matt's look struck him also.
He wondered if he himself were in the way.
Would these two rather have gone on that long
ridge walk together ?

Might there be a knight's move that would be
required of him presently, — one square off, and
two squares down ?

This walk was his at any rate ; it could not be
helped now ; and Jane had certainly looked glad.
He would be as fair to himself as to another ; and
then, — he could be generous, — if he were sure
that it would be generous to Jane.

It brought his own thought to a focus ; he knew
now, if he had not known before, what he would
do, if he could do it in his own undoubted right.

So they went up the ridge together ; a fair world
about them ; the same pleasant things in the same
pathway for the two ; a moment ago an unspoken
unison between them, that only waited interpreta-

tion to fuse what was, as yet, separate in but half-analyzed happiness, to conscious, acknowledged, authorized joy; it had been like daydawn without a cloud; but now a mist had rolled over; it was not sure that there could come a visible sunrise.

Jane knew that she had, in a certain way, put herself in a false position; it was something so slight, so inappreciable, that there was no such thing as setting it right; it was irrevocable because of its shadowiness. Oh! why should her embarrassment have made her blush? Why could she not have taken the simple things simply? Why should it seem of consequence to her? — a consequence likely to be interpreted precisely wrong. She was vexed; she was ashamed; so her embarrassment continued.

It was not in her nature to be rude, ungrateful; yet she could have thrown the little bunch of leaves away. Only that would do no good; it would prove nothing, except, indeed, it might italicize, as with false, evasive act, the consciousness that looked like proof already. So she carried it clasped in her left hand that dropped down by her side; and it was as if nettles stung her.

Little things had annoyed her before. Things that could not be avoided or contradicted; there had been little looks in Mistress Margaret's face that Jane, with all her love, resented. Mrs. Sunderland was thinking, perhaps, — it might be they were all thinking, planning, — how something should befall which they were arranging in their own minds was to be good for her — for Jane. And what she was most. indignant with was her own indignation; what she was most bitterly abased by was her own mortification. Of what had she been thinking, that she should be angry that they could think of this? Such a mere remoteness, too; a thing that had had no time to begin to be.

What other remoteness, impossibility, was there, that had begun to be in the way for Jane?

It was by no means clear to her, as I make it, writing it down; she would not have let it be. But in her mingled feeling it threatened her with its demand; it drove her to precisely the same conclusion, in a shrinking, momentary perception, that the doctor had come to by an insight a man need not be ashamed to face.

She would think of nothing; she would fear nothing; she would not challenge or misdoubt herself. She would take this walk with her friend as he had asked her, for her good. After all, there is no reassurance like that which comes in the safety of being suspected of exactly the wrong thing.

It was an air and scene in which all little circumstantial shackles might fall off. The keen, clear wind, tempered with such sunny warmth as

only the lingering of the real summer in her sweetest places gives, when she meets the rich, luxurious
advance of her Indian sister, and the two reign on
together, as they do sometimes, and as they did
this year, swept up around them, full of stimulus
and fragrance, seeming to lift and bear away whatever might oppress, perplex, or fret; replacing
doubt or discomfort with buoyancy and placid
strength. Peace and vigor were the elements of
the atmosphere ; it wrapped the body with a life
that penetrated and reinforced the very inmost
being. It was all so large, so gracious ; one could
take in without stint such satisfying that uncontent
fell back, rebuked. " How shall He not freely
give us all things?" the spirit cried, rejoicing.
And nothing seemed impossible to be or to come,
when all this was here, a whole horizon flooded and
brimmed with ecstasies, to make one transcendent
hour for just two human souls.

It was not without knowledge and foresight that
Dr. Griffith had so spoken, — "To do her good."
He knew how she had been cramped and limited ;
he wanted to bring her out into these large places,
to see their effect upon her ; they would measure
her with themselves. How fully would she — could
she — receive and hold ?

The inland side of the ridge was here a long,
rough slope ; they went up over crisp, short turf,

broken with outcrops of stone, where flat little
juniper bushes spread their blue-green branches,
and clung; the goldenrods stood up in flaming
beauty, every spire an exuberant bloom, of a plu-
miness and softness such as Jane had never seen
before; and the little, pale, starry asters clustered
among them, smiling up to their glory, as saying,
" We are less, — we differ, — but we shine, our way,
too ! "

"I think they talk to each other," Jane said,
catching the word of it as she stooped among them
and gathered some of the bright and lovely things,
which she put with the leaf-cluster.   It was not all
Matt Morse's now; she was more comfortable with
it.

There was a good deal of tacit language about;
Dr. Griffith translated a small syllable from this,
that made him more inwardly content.

They came up on the crest; they faced the sea,
that swept up so grandly into the bosom of the
land, parting the hills into islands, and afar off
stretching in its own infinity to the remotest southerly touch of the bending sky.

Backward, they looked among the heights of a
green country; opposite shores, eastward, rose in
grand inclines; yet they knew that all around and
among them ran the strong, deep channels, and
that the tides sent up their mighty pulsations between fields and forests, for miles and miles.

" How wonderful it is, the hills and the sea rushing together like this ! " said Jane.   " I have been
on a flat beach, before; then it seemed to come to an
end, both ways ; the shore had run to a sandy edge,
and the sea had come to its long line that it could
not cross; but here — why, it is both conquering
and making triumph together ! "

She seldom said so much ; it was the pressure of
the fullness upon her ; there was that in her which
must speak, so borne upon.

She gazed out upon the mingled splendor of
land and water, in a flush of many colors, inde-
scribably rich and lovely : the deep evergreens holding their summer verdure ; the clumps of yellow
birches ; the scattered oaks and maples, burning
in their crimson and orange ; the scarlet tongues
of vine and shrub, shooting and waving here and
there with vivid flashes as of fire ; the great, changing, many-hued ocean, opaline under the bright sky
and shifting cloud-shadows, — all this to the eye,
while the sweet, keen breeze carried the strength
and joy of it to the very life-centre ; how could she
but forget everything — herself most of all — as
she stood there, in an amaze of gladness ?

Dr. Griffith looked at her ; she, in this new environment, was his especial study ; yet the same
great spell was upon him also ; the intense delight
was the being in that same wondrous world —

really lifted into it and its sublime meanings — in companionship.

"I think you prescribed for more than you knew, Dr. Griffith," Jane said, as presently they walked on again along the cliff. "I think the 'good' reaches further than breath or eyesight."

"It is a poor physician who treats only for the external," Dr. Griffith returned. "I knew pretty well what this would be to you. How far have you ever been in this direction?"

"Not any distance at all. I wasn't sure of the climbing for the children."

"I shall show you new things, then. Are you sure-footed?"

Jane laughed. "I have never been tried very much, you know, off the sidewalks. But I think I have a steady head."

Down at their left plunged the broken fissured rocks; at their base curled and hissed the fringing waters; on the other side the slope grew continually more precipitous, as the reef-like promontory reached on southwesterly; the narrow, rutted road was lost in the thick undergrowth and below the impending height; across the lessening strip of land could be seen the blue glimmer of the inlet westward, and the thickly shaded shores of the larger, farther island township.

They had to cross a high, sharp neck that was

little more than a pathway, and part of it a scramble across and between the jags of rock.

Dr. Griffith took her hand at perilous points, or such as might have been so in weather less serene, or for a hasty step, or an easily dizzied head. Jane proved her head to be steady, as she had said; and her feet took firm, well-poised hold where the cool head discerned the safest way.

They went up as far as they could along the summit; then the doctor led her down, carefully, into a steep ravine that cleft the headland. They came, at length, to a broadened shelf that nearly closed the fissure from side to side, while forward the passage flared suddenly open upon the face of the ledge, and they were confronted with the sea. Behind them reared the rocks they had descended; the country landscape had disappeared; they were held in a mountain recess, alone before the majesty of ocean.

" Now you can sit and rest; you are absolutely sheltered here," said Dr. Griffith, as he spread a shawl upon a jut of rock where she could lean luxuriously against the cliff-side. " Do you know you are above the lighthouse ? "

" I think — I am above and beyond everything," said Jane slowly.

Dr. Griffith seated himself near by.

They were utterly silent then, for many minutes.

He met Jane in the doorway, and gave them to her. Margaret came forth upon the instant. " *Those* — at this time in the year ! " she exclaimed.

" If you know how to look," said Dr. Griffith.

> "'For those who have souls to perceive,
> The violets bloom in October! ' "

" I think they only grew for you," said his sister.

" No ; for they are not mine now," he returned.

And Jane said nothing. But she presently went away with her flowers ; and it seemed suddenly as if the very refusal of her life that had been so hard to understand had put forth a disclosure of graciousness in flush and fragrance.

" To-morrow, if this beautiful weather holds," said Dr. Griffith, as they met on the cottage green at tea-time, " we go to Pemaquid. And it will hold. Look at the sky. We must use every day, now, and lose nothing. We will drain every drop of this wonderful pleasure."

He spoke like a boy, in his brimful delight. Somehow his doubts had got put by.

Jane smiled.

" What is it, Miss Gregory ? " he asked her. " There 's a meaning in your look — as there 's apt to be."

" Only," she said, " that I think it would be like

the autocrat's syrup pitcher. You couldn't drain it dry, if you held it upside down a thousand years."

"Yes, you are right. That is the wonder of it. And we won't turn it upside down!"

So they went in to tea.

Afterward, Matt Morse came up. He brought the mails, and reported Ladybird as lying ready in the little Sandy Cove.

Then he asked Dr. Griffith to go down with him and see that all was right on board.

"I wanted to have a word with you," the young man said, as soon as they got upon the little beach. "I want to know something."

"All right," answered the doctor, standing still, and bracing himself involuntarily against what might be coming.

"It is about Miss Gregory. I want to know how much she is above me."

"That I can't tell, Matt, until I know better how high you are."

"I don't mean that way. I mean in the world."

"In the world, Miss Gregory is simply a young girl who maintains herself by her own efforts."

"I am glad of it," said Matt honestly. "But it's the way now for young women to do that. She might be out of my reach, all the same. Are her relations people who would — think there was n't any world outside theirs, except for them to travel in, in summer-time ? "

"She has no immediate relatives at all. My sister tells me that she is quite alone."

Matthew stood up in a fine manly strength. " She sha'n't be that much longer, Dr. Griffith, if she will listen to me."

That was plain enough.

John Griffith made the knight's move.

" My friend," he said, " there is nothing in the way, that I know of, except brief knowledge, and a woman's reserve of herself for the truest there can be for her.   If you think you can show her that, it is your chance to try."

The categorical, matter-of-fact fashion of the doctor's answers struck Matt — for he was quick enough — with a sense of something near the truth.

" It is your chance to try," he said.

After that, it might be some one else would try. The doctor by no means cared if this did appear ; though he would not willfully have made it patent by the least phrase or tone.

Matthew Morse should have his rights.   These days were his only opportunity ; afterward — well Dr. Griffith could not be so sure of afterwards, of course, holding himself back now, at the possible crisis.

What should hinder a girl like Jane, fresh in

her joy of this free life, thrown into companionship with a brave, handsome, loving young fellow who was a king in this realm of nature, from seeing all that was fine and strong in him, all that was beautiful in the grand simplicity of the world she could marry herself into, taking him? Why, an English duchess could not come into more superb surroundings of estate than a woman whose virtual domain should be all that she could appreciate and take to herself among these hills and waters, beneath these glorious wide skies.

What position would Dr. Griffith place himself in, pausing now? If these days were Matthew Morse's, where were his own?

They were where they had been in the two years between his first meeting this woman of such fair womanliness and his finding her again.

They were as safe as those, if they were days meant for him; since now he willfully missed nothing, but simply had to make his knight's move, and stand aside a bit in generous honor.

Yet it was very like that turning of his pitcher upside down, which he had said he would not do.

It was after dark when he came into the little parlor of the cottage. And then he looked over his letters; said he must go to his room and answer them, that he might have a holiday to-morrow; advised his sister to keep early hours; and so they all said good-night.

The morrow was a fair, rich day; not much wind, but what there was, was westerly; it would do. Nobody was in a hurry. They were to be on the water for pleasure, and the sail would be none too long.

"We are idle folks," Margaret said. "We came here to drift; we don't want too much energy in anything."

Aunt Kreeshy stored the little cabin, which was hardly more than a cubby and a locker, with her good things: her bread and butter and cold chicken, her apple pie, her bottled coffee and cream, her brown, spicy doughnuts and sage cheese.

They were going up around Southport, to be as little out at sea as possible this first trial trip, and to enjoy the beautiful, gradual coming out among the islands.

All went but Aunty, whose physical as well as mental constitution was a protest against any kind of wee-waws. Miss Rickstack was in that condition of courage and high spirits which comes from daring one sort of similar risk when quite incapable of another; as some people will ride with great exhilaration behind two horses, who dare not go at all with one. She "supposed it was going to sea in a bowl, after all," she said. "But it wasn't a *saucer*, which made all the difference. There was some sort of a fence to keep you and the sea separate." Aunt Kreeshy went because "it come so she could as well as not," and to help them with their lunch.

The sweet, soft breeze would be gently in their favor nearly all the way; and they would come back with the tide.

In the east cut, for a little while, even the slight wind they had would be shut off from them; but Matt Morse knew how to manage, and he was not loth to have it to do. Old Captain Zenas and a boy were his sufficient crew; there would be leisure for him to use this day's "chance" for himself. Yet he did not want all leisure; his very command was his opportunity; like every sailor, he was twice a man on board his vessel. If there had been just a little more need for seamanship he would have liked it better; to-day there was only the mere prettiness of light, easy handling, for the most part.

But this passage through the cut called for strength and alertness, in the way Matt accomplished 'it, which few possessed as he did, or could manifest with an equal certainty and skill. Perhaps his advice to take the northward round, bringing them down through this inlet, was not wholly unbiased by the pleasure of putting forth his prowess before the eyes that would be looking on.

One side here was a sheer face of rock; on the

other, a strip of woods edged the river; back of this rose steeply the cliff, fringed with hemlocks and birches; between, the stream ran slow and deep; it looked still and black, under the overhanging shadows; only the oaks and maples lit the gorge with any color, lifting their bright heads above the wild undergrowth which wrapped their feet in a dull green.

Matt Morse sprang ashore with a long leap, carrying with him one end of a heavy rope that was fastened at the other to the boat's bow.

"How did he get there?" exclaimed Miss Rickstack, first catching sight of him on land as he plunged along the tangled, broken foothold of stems and stones among which he had alighted as he could.

Aunt Kreeshy had never happened to see him perform this exploit before. "You can't *do* it, Matt," she cried, with a sharp, rising inflection, "no *more 'n* a hen can wash dishes."

The ignominious comparison drew a shout of laughter from the boat party, as Matt gave the contradiction by his agile springs and swings, past and around the crowding tree boles; now up and now down the bank wherever he could perch or grasp; flinging his rope ahead, and keeping it free and straight to the yacht, till he had gained such distance that he could throw the line around some sturdy trunk, and send the loose end by a sure flight from a strong, steady hand, back on board, where it was caught and hauled upon, warping the craft forward from point to point.

Sometimes, for a little clearer way, making the rope's turn around his own body, he would go sturdily on, towing the vessel; then take it in hand to thread again an intricate, steep place; springing across the breaks from rock to rock, climbing around obstacles, flashing in and out of sight like a squirrel, never losing his quick calculation, never missing aim; till just at the right moment, down below, where wood and cliff sloped to open shore again, he made the last bend and haul, and as the boat slid inward to\ ard him, leaped on board, flushed, handsome, c ,reless, and unspent.

Before they had traced; his last movement, he was with them, and had sat down by Jane. Aunt Kreeshy was on the other side.

"It's all fair and easy now," Matt said. "She 'll go along of herself — all she can make of it."

"You 've got good wind," said aunt Kreeshy.

"Do you call this good wind? Baby's breath. For my part, I 'd rather beat a little."

"No baby's breath about it. I said *you* had got good wind," repeated aunt Kreeshy.

"Oh, I. Bound to have, you know, when Lady-bird could n't catch hers. I like to give a good pull through a hard place."

"It 's good when can and will go together. Guess they most always do with you, Matt."

Aunt Kreeshy had no boy of her own, and she was very proud and fond of the young boatman. Whatever else she may have had in her head, praising him now, she thought was her own secret, even when she added, with innocent simplicity, "I don't believe *any* lady-bird o' your'n ever 'll have to tug alone through the tough spots."

Might it have been apropos to that, or to divert slightly the too personal subject, that Matthew be-gan to tell them of the new yacht he had nearly finished for a rich cottager at Squirrel Island?

The Windflower, he said it was to be called.

And then he went on to speak of further plans: in a few years, he said he believed he could take on men enough, and run a big business; and not need to leave home for it, either.

"Oh, I should n't think you would ever want to leave home!" Jane exclaimed.

Matthew turned to her with a bright face. "You like it here so much?" he asked.

Jane's day had begun with such a fullness of in-ward joy that it would last far on with her. She had not noticed yet any withdrawal or interruption; she had had so much that she would even rather wait; and her glad content was ready to overflow without constraint. She forgot to be jealous of herself with Matt. "Oh, yes!" she cried. "I think it must be a great love to anybody that lets them be born here!"

"That's a real pretty way of sayin' it, an' pious too," commented aunt Kreeshy kindly. The little secret thought in her own mind was freshly commending itself all the time to her judgment. "Maybe that's why the Lord brings some people here that was n't born here, too," she added, with satisfaction. And with transparent artifice she changed her seat to a little down the bench, pretending to turn and look over at something on the water.

Matthew was too much in earnest to say any flippant, presuming thing, such as very likely he had spoken to other pretty girls upon occasion. It was no time to say a serious thing, that might precipitate a displeasure; so he was silent.

Jane was simply thinking that it was indeed God's love that had given her these days; and that she did not say, of course. She sat still, and half forgot her companion.

The absolute serenity of her face charmed Matthew; it awed him likewise. How was a girl like this to be approached, persuaded, in ordinary fashion?

CHAPTER XIII

MARGARET spoke suddenly to Jane from the other side of the boat. They were not ten feet apart.

"Oh, you ought to hear this, Queen ! Uncle Hans is telling us how Pemaquid came near being Boston, and Boston nowhere."

Uncle Hans had a child on each knee. On either side of him sat his sister and Miss Rickstack. Speaking thus across, Mrs. Sunderland made the two groups one ; of course, they were the more so, being opposite, than they could have been all on one side. Certainly, nobody had reason for discontent. If Jane were a wee bit happier, summoned into the other conversation, than she had been a moment before, she scarcely needed to be.

Dr. Griffith explained how it was once called "Jamestown," for the English king, contemporaneously with Jamestown in Virginia ; that it was the capital of New England, before Boston was at all ; and how indignant the people were at being tacked on to Massachusetts and losing their importance ; how Pemaquid fell back to its Indian name, and its buildings dropped into decay, and its paved streets got covered up, and how they tell you now about a " buried city ; " but that as to how much of it is really buried underground, and how much only in time and forgetfulness, he could not say.

" I never heard of it in my life before ! " cried Mrs. Sunderland.

" Suppose it had been the other way," said Jane.

" That Boston had got buried up, and that here had grown up the commerce, and the great city, and the learning and the splendor ? And that the Three Hills had been called to-day just Shawmut ; and the waters ran all in and around, and Back Bay was not made into solid ground ; but little boats, like this, with pleasuring people from this proud old Jamestown, sailed back and forth there between forest banks, in a stillness like this ? "

" One *can't* imagine it," said Margaret.

> " ' A thousand years shall pass, and then
> I mean to go that way again,' "

quoted Dr. Griffith. " Ah ! where shall we be in the thousand years ? "

" I almost think that Pemaquid is the happiest," said Jane. " I *almost* wish that all the cities could be buried, and the world kept fresh, and the work and the pleasure divided round, without such a festering first."

"Yes, it is a festering in one way. It grows unhealthy. Everything is excessive. It taxes men's nerves and souls to live in it."

"What do you think of the *women*," asked Margaret, "who have the details of life? Do you know what a day's shopping is, now that you have ten miles to go and do it, and towers of Babel to do it in?"

"Even the horse-car conductors seem to have it on their consciences," said Jane, with a funny little smile. "Don't you know what they say, when they cry out the two big bazaar stores and the crush corners, as they come to them, and let out their own jam on Washington Street?"

"No; how do you mean?"

"'*Ah*, — Wretch, — Wh—y? — *Chawed'n* — Mashed! — Winter — *and* — Summer!'"

Jane mimicked it gently, with just a touch of street-car intonation.

"They call it out, over and over, every trip; and yet the women swarm and crowd, and never notice the remonstrance. I've often wondered that they didn't."

"*I* shall always notice it after this," cried Margaret, laughing delightedly. "It's capital!" And then, with more little laughs between the words, she repeated them, and translated to aunt Kreeshy their parody upon the names of the great firms and the street crossings where the wildest tussle and roar go on perpetually — " ' winter *and* summer.' Jane, you demure thing, where do you generally keep all the fun that is in you?"

"Maybe where my good times are," Jane answered.

Jane was in a good time now, then. Her face was merry. Little ripples of freshening content played over it as she lifted it to the pleasant air. The soft fawn-brown locks fluttered lightly upon her forehead; her eyes were full of light.

How much of this was of the moment? How much belonged to Matthew Morse?

These questions put themselves to John Griffith, as he looked on, studying so much deeper than the jest that he scarcely smiled at it. Jane wondered at his gravity. She was afraid she had been a little silly, even out of taste, with her mimicry. The first faint breath of chill came over her perfect day. How could she, on the one part, guess what the grave look meant? And how could Dr. Griffith, on the other, understand that yesterday had flowed over into to-day, and that Matthew Morse simply in the reflex light of it?

he real history of the remaining hours was in gs that cannot be written. Matt got the best ., as matters seemed; he had plenty of opporty. Dr. Griffith gave him his chance, and

Jane allowed him what she certainly could not put herself voluntarily in the way for, elsewhere.

It was Matt who told her, as they sailed between Mouse Island and Boothbay, with Squirrel Island off at their right, southward, how the splendid surf came up on the Squirrel Rocks over beyond the sweet cedar woods; who pointed out dim Damariscove, and said they would go out there some day; who showed her beautiful Spruce Point, darkly dense with evergreens, that in spring were all tasseled with bright, new tips, like dropping gold; who reminded her, as they rounded Ocean Point, that here they were fairly out on the Atlantic, that fifteen miles off there, to the east, was old Monhegan, and just northwest, before them, was Pemaquid; and that all the way from here to Passamaquoddy lay crowds of beautiful islands, with capes and points and bays and inlets, and innumerable windings, and quiet harbors and land-locked river mouths behind them, in the grand ragged shore that measures four degrees of longitude, and which enchanted with its primeval loveliness the brave Northmen who came down from Iceland five hundred years before Columbus sailed from Spain, and in between Cape Sable and Cape Cod found this, to them, fair southern coast, and named it Vinland.

I am bound to say that Matthew not only had a

good chance, but that he used it well. Jane could not help being charmed with all that he was telling her. She did not let herself be impatient that she could not have everything at once. She was far too unpretending to expect continual personal notice and kindness from Mrs. Sunderland and her brother, — that was how she put it to herself, — or to be always in their inner circle of companionship. A pleasant word or glance, when it did come, reassured her, even as to the momentary gravity which had troubled her awhile since, foolishly, she thought ; for how could she suppose that Dr. Griffith might not have plenty to preoccupy his mind, and prevent his entering into every little nonsense she, or anybody else, might utter ? Yet the day had a little longer stretch in it for her as the noon drew on.

They had their early lunch, and were gay over it. Aunt Kreeshy did the honors, and took the whole trouble. The children skipped back and forth, and spun the company all into one web again. Afterward, Jane got Rick and Alice to her, with Miss Rickstack, and began a game.

They were a long time working up from Ocean Point. The slight breeze deserted them, and the tide was at low slack water. Matthew got out his long sweep, and now at one side, now at the other, was urging his vessel with stalwart strokes, only to hold her own, it seemed. She scarcely gained perceptible headway.

Dr. Griffith offered help ; but whether Matthew had a second sweep or not, he did not produce it. He was used, he said, to one-man power. Evidently, it was his innings again.

The doctor made his sister comfortable for a rest in a small sea-chair, and came and stood by the others, busy with their game of " Twenty Questions." He knew better than to keep too obviously apart. There was no reason why, like Matthew with his oar, he should not, at least, hold the distance he had won. He need not drift quite out to sea, though he had taken down his sail.

Miss Rickstack had been set to guess. The questions she propounded had already counted up to forty. She was making wild rushes up and down all time and around all creation with her discursive inquiry, the children in high glee, meanwhile, at her futile surmises and the cleverness of Jane in having made suggestion of such a good " object."

" May I come in and help ? " asked the doctor, when he had listened for a while.

" Oh, you 'll finish it right up ! " cried Alice. " But you may."

" See, Jane, how quick uncle Hans will get at whatever he sets out for." And the small maiden clapped her hands in anticipated triumph.

Uncle Hans recounted the points they had thus far made.

" It is an animal, and small and soft; not particularly useful; ornamental ? "

" Oh, *very!* " said Alice. " That's one question."

" I *guessed* a muff," said Miss Rickstack complacently.

" Oh, but that *is* useful! " said Alice. " And it is n't ' a ' anything. It is always one particular thing."

" Ancient or modern ? " asked the doctor.

" Modern," Jane answered, for he looked at her.

" Alive ? "

" Yes."

" Can't be Alice's nose ? Is it in this part of the world ? "

" It is."

" In Leeport ? "

" Yes."

" Domestic or wild ? "

" Domestic."

" Belongs to Mrs. Morse ? "

" It does."

" Is it a whole animal, or a part of one ? "

" A part."

" A small point, or an important part ? "

" A small point."

At which the children shrieked, and Dr. Griffith guessed, in a tumult of applause, —

" The white spot on the tip of aunt Kreeshy's black cat's tail."

" I *never* sàw such a guesser, or such a noticer ! " exclaimed Alice.

Dr. Griffith gave her ear a little pinch, and walked away to seat himself at the rudder with old Captain Zenas.

A puff of wind had risen again. The sail was run up, and filled ; they slipped smoothly over the placid, sunny water, and so came presently to Pemaquid.

Here, I am forced to confess, the holiday turned a bit dull. The interest of Pemaquid was in the fact of it, and this they had enjoyed beforehand. There was not much here to be seen ; only the small patches and vestiges of what had once begun to be, and the very quiet and ordinary presentment of what had actually come to pass.

It was Matthew Morse again who helped Jane to land, and who walked about with her and Miss Rickstack, as they viewed the fragmentary traces of the ancient town and fort. Mrs. Sunderland was soon tired, and went back on board, where aunt Kreeshy was taking her comfortable knitting-and-dozing spell, as if she had been in her own kitchen at home. Dr. Griffith accompanied his

sister, and read to her from some new story, while
the children remained with the shore party.

Jane was not sorry when the word was given for
all to return. The remaining hours of sunshine
would be none too many for the outward sail determined on, and the reaching home as early as com-
patible with the benefit of the tide up through the
bay. The wind had freshened and gone a point to
the northward. It had a keener touch, but there
was no harshness in it, and the unclouded sun sent
streaming warmth along the waters.

It was a lovely afterpart; the most beautiful bit
of the day was this, when the light began to fall
slantwise, and the sea turned violet and green and
pearl color, stretching out under the softening sky.
Backward, the land rose in radiant heights, the
hills standing in autumn sheen that, evening after
evening, now sent challenge to the sunsets across
the liquid deep that reflected and repeated, or
gave softening and blending neutral tints between.

Jane was still with the pleasure of beholding;
perhaps with purpose also, since again Matt and
aunt Kreeshy were beside her. The children were
quiet from some beginning of weariness. With
little ulsters buttoned close, they cuddled upon
cushions on the deck between their mother and
Miss Rickstack.

Dr. Griffith had covered his sister carefully with

shawls, and placed her chair so that her face was from the sun and the warmth was upon her shoulders; he himself stood gazing off beyond the outer islands, upon the pearl and beryl shimmer of the southerly expanse.

They were on the long tack outward. Matthew need not be very busy with the boat; he began to talk again with aunt Kreeshy of his hopes and plans. Poor fellow, he had to crowd a little, for his time was short!

"One of these days," he said, "I'll build a cottage for myself on Button Island. I'm my own land company there, you know, and I mean to stay so. It is as good growing value for me as for anybody, and a pretty little house won't hurt it. I'll have nothing but a house and a garden and a boatyard. There isn't a nicer bit of land and water in the whole bay."

"And what'll father do?"

"Father'll go where I go. The farm can be let out, or the land sold some time. It's getting heavy for him, and my boat-building ought to be the best craft of the two. The garden will be just pretty work for him to see to. Yes, father'll go where I go."

It was manly of him to repeat this. He meant to let his filial duty be plainly understood. That lost no ground for him, if he had any, with Jane;

she only thought the talk was turning more on family matters than it concerned her to hear. What was Button Island to her?

She wondered if she might not get up and walk away. Would it be rude, a rebuke to Matthew's forwardness with his own affairs, if she did so? Would the quiet person standing there, sending his thoughts away from all of them along that seaward beauty take heed at all if she should? Would he have any word for her to-day, or ever any more, such as he had given her? How far off was yesterday? She was so silent that her silence fell, presently, upon the others.

"The boom, Miss Gregory!"

She hardly knew how long it had been, or that Matthew had left his place to attend to his sail, or had said a word of cautioning reminder as he did so, when the canvas flapped in the wind, the heavy spar swung round, and Dr. Griffith's voice and hand reached her just in time.

Then, for a moment, he did stay beside her. What reason was there for his visibly neglecting her?

"Have you had a good day?" he asked her. "Are you tired?"

"The day has been wonderful. I could never be tired of the hills and the sea," Jane answered.

Was it in instinctive use of that hidden weapon

of defensive coquetry with which woman nature, however sweet and true, is armed, that, feeling his tone, she added what she did?

"I shall be sorry to leave them. I would like to be among them always."

With how much of a mere man's feeling, and with how much of his real, large kindliness and faith did he answer her?

"I hope you will always have the best you can have ; and I believe you will," he said.

"You believe that for everybody, don't you, Dr. Griffith ?"

"In a sense, yes. But we all miss, or put off, a great deal that we might have. It is held right out to us, but we are blind, or do not care. That is why it has taken the world a hundred millions of years to get where it even is to-day," he added, with a sudden generalizing.

"Shall we go round and round a hundred millions of years before we get at even the whole of ourselves ?" Jane asked the question as it rose in her mind, but not as one who expects an answer.

"I suppose 'the patience of the saints' is the sure waiting of them who are being 'sainted,' which is simply being made whole," said Dr. Griffith.

With just those words, he made her and her day rich again.

But would such words, such days, come only once, or twice, or twenty times in the round of her appointed years? How many rounds would there have to be before that healing, that whole-making, should come to her, to which every leaf upon the tree of life at last shall minister for the nations?

How much had she done herself, just now, to possibly put such things by?

This man who " guessed," who " noticed," everything — what had she given him now to think?

But she could not get back her words.

If her day ended in a gift, it hardly ended in a gladness.

CHAPTER XIV.

" I THINK it looks as if there were a place making here on purpose for Jane," said Mrs. Sunderland to her brother.

" Do you wish it ? " asked Dr. Griffith.

" I am very fond of Jane. I wish her to be very happy, and I think it seems possible here and suitable."

" Suitable to what ? "

" To Jane herself, and her position."

" Ah, Margaret ! Ascutney Street ! "

" John, you *know* I have n't any of that sort of feeling about it ! "

" Do I ? Do you ? "

" If you mean that I don't like things unsuitable, you can quote Ascutney Street, if you like," said Margaret with dignity. " I feel responsible for Jane ; and I shall be glad if all goes well for her, in a safe, rational way. I can't help loving the girl, and I don't want to be the means of turning her head."

" Margaret," said Dr. Griffith, gravely and quietly, " I can't help loving the girl, either."

Margaret flushed up, very red, and sat silent.

" May I speak right out, Gretel ? " he asked her kindly.

" To me ? I think you have. What else is there ? "

" Only this : that I want the best of you in league with what I know is the best of me. Your class training is in the way just now. Theoretically, you deny it, even to yourself. Practically, it is troubling you."

" Because I think I may have made a great mistake."

" It 's just here, Gretel. The mistake is not in what you have done, but in what you may do. Women of your sort are always falling into precisely such dilemmas. You take up people for what they are; at a certain point you set them down again because of what they are rated to be. Your patronage becomes caprice, because it ought never to have been patronage, but pure recognition."

It was somewhat hard for Margaret, who thought she had recognized with some generosity, to be told this.

" And what do men of your sort do ? " she asked.

" What God — not the Devil — puts it into a man's heart to do."

Margaret looked up at John with eyes full of love, but trouble also.

"I do not mean to be proud," she said, "and I could not be proud against you ; but what if this — a simple life in the midst of all she delights in so with her whole nature — were the right thing?"

"That is what I am waiting to see. But when you speak of her whole nature, Margaret, I doubt if it is met here. She is higher than Matthew Morse."

"And you are higher than she. Why should not a man marry up, as well as a woman?"

"There is no why not. Both must marry up."

"How can that be?"

"I am speaking of the Kingdom of Heaven. Gretel, we must go behind the looking-glass in these things. There is an inside world; it is there that God joins together. If people marry in the outside world and for it, they make a sham, — a reflection, thin and evanescent. They are nothing but shadows to each other ; not even true images at that. I must go behind the shadows. I must find my wife in the certain-true."

"And yet you are waiting for this other thing to happen, if it will?"

"Yes. It could only begin to happen now, I suppose. It is too soon. But she is going away. I think he will say something. I shall give him his opportunity."

It was on Margaret's mind to ask, "Why do you not give her her choice?" But it did not get to her lips. She really did not know that it would be right. Jane was a good girl; but a good girl may be dazzled by very goodness. This question must be settled by heart-instinct, not by any enthusiasm of admiration, any glamour of upward looking. John knew best. Matthew's chance had better come first. She could not wish against her brother; but she still thought he might be saved from a mistake. If he were, he would be saved completely, after some struggle, perhaps. He was strong and good. He would not let this spoil his life.

"On Wednesday, or Thursday, we go to Wiscasset," said Dr. Griffith, after the pause in which she had been thinking this. "If we make out Wiscasset on Wednesday, then I will run up on Thursday and see that all is ready at Bay Hill. I shall be back on Saturday. You will want my help here the day before you leave."

The subject was changed. Margaret could not return to it. There were a dozen questions she would have liked to ask, but it was not time for them yet.

Their answers hung upon what might happen in this week to come.

Jane had time, before the Wednesday, to ask

herself many questions — growing rapidly more definite and searching — in which no one else could help her.

Where was the happy looking-forward gone that she had had thus far in every fresh plan and promise, in every day for the next day to come? Why had Pemaquid been disappointing, and why did she think of beautiful Wiscasset and this new sail up and down the river-aisles with a certain dread?

The catechizing came close home. Whatever other people meant, what did she mean herself? Why had kindness — it was only that — from one person made the same sort of kindness irksome to her from anybody else? Why was the least withdrawal painful to her, on the one side; the least advance repugnant to her, on the other? *Was* it the same sort of kindness? Had she any right to call the two the same? Why was she so quick to fear from the one, so slow to hope from the other?

To hope what? What absurd presumption was she beginning to be guilty of?

She would prove to herself that it was nothing. She would keep herself in a tight hold. She would let one thing be as another. She would not be afraid. She would not be disappointed. She would take things as they came. How foolish otherwise! How soon it would all be over! What could it possibly amount to in these few days left? They would all go back again, away from these woods and waters; they would never see Matt Morse any more. Dr. Griffith would go home to Sunnywater.

One thing sent a pulse of exultation through her as she thought of it. Mrs. Sunderland was her friend; she belonged with her; she would hear; she would know; there would be a link; she should not altogether lose —

What?

She brought herself short up again with the stern demand. If they could think of this as further kindness, what did it make of her — desiring to keep — not bearing to lose? Pride and shame flamed up in her.

What right had she to let a single imagination stray out beyond Mrs. Sunderland and her service? Least of all, through her to hers, who only as hers could be of any distant concern to herself, Jane Gregory? It was base; it was disingenuous; it was not to be allowed. If she could not help this, she must go away to her seamstressing again; she must go back to Ascutney Street.

Holding this threat over herself, she shaped her behavior.

Every day that our little party planned for seemed also planned to meet them, with all concomitants of wind and weather. Wednesday came with a sweet, south, summer air. The atmosphere was balm. It was a golden day of a golden season. Going up the river their sails were full. It was only as the stream and inlets wound about that their course involved a little shifting. It was just enough to escape monotony.

Captain Zenas could not go to-day. Matthew had more to do, therefore. A part of the time Dr. Griffith sat at the tiller. When Matthew took it from him, he asked Jane if she would not like to steer. How could any one suppose that her ready assent was in pure contradiction of herself? That because she would really rather have been somewhere else, she seated herself with Matthew in the stern, the tiller-shaft between them, and with good will took her lesson?

Not Matthew; he was blithe. Not Dr. Griffith; he saw as a man sees, — even so keen a man as Dr. Griffith, — where it stands him in closest behoof to be keen. For Margaret Sunderland, a woman with a little sympathetic, innocent feminine crookedness, it was the first glimpse toward the truth.

All this day she watched. It was *noblesse oblige* with her. Because she had not been quite able to wish that her brother might do this thing, because she knew that, if the other happened, she would be secretly half relieved, — or would have

been before that talk with Hans, — she set herself
to see clearly, even in Hans' behalf.

Through the nobility of this very contrariety of
her own, she discerned the contrariety in Jane.
Does a generous person reach out an eager hand
to seize the best thing, the thing most unquestion-
ably to be desired? Does a delicate woman put
herself forth to take with over-readiness that which
her hidden hope most covets, or does she half avert
herself and put it by, letting some commoner claim
and opportunity assert itself, that the " thing so
sweet, so dear," may not know its own great price,
but may come insisting, if it will come at all?

How far, possibly, might this go? How far
was it a consciousness? With her brother standing aloof, — the very fact, perhaps, awakening Jane
to what she would be self-shamed to realize, —
might it even be that she should be drawn into
this easier possibility, to cure herself of the first,
that was so preposterous, so hopeless?

" I want the best of you to be in league with
what I know is the best of me." That was what
John had said. It repeated itself over and over
again to Margaret now.

Jane got a little tired of Matthew, apart from
whatever Matthew's seeking and lingering might
mean. He was somewhat too content, to-day, perhaps; he was slipping into that easy assurance that

had grown to be his habit from the way in which his world had treated him; it began, maybe, to seem easy enough to enter, if he would, this other.

He talked a little too much of his own life, plans, and resources. In the midst of this wider, finer delight — this outlook upon river, hills, and heaven that they had come for, in which might have been read to her, Jane knew, such wonderful sentences of a living word — little personal hopes and prides seemed trivial, obtrusive. She grew silent and did not listen to quite all he said. It looked like listening, though, and Dr. Griffith interpreted it as contentment, if not pleasure. Margaret detected, in the still face the shade of weariness, the line of endurance.

So they sailed past the sprinkling islands and up the beautiful straits, through the long, deep dale of the Sheepscote between Upper Westport and Edgecombe on the east, and came into bright Wiscasset Bay.

Jane got the children with her, a part of the time, after their lunch; but she could not even cling to them without seeming to cling to their more special surrounding; and uncle Hans was never spared from their monopoly long. She began to tell them a story, and they called to him to come and hear. Then she brought it to its climax quickly, and Rick rebelled.

"They *did n't* go home and live happy ever after, right then. You've skipped!" he cried resentfully.

"Have I?" Jane said, a little listlessly. "I'll tell it all over again, by-and-by."

"Miss Gregory is tired," said Dr. Griffith. "Come away. We are going to haul up to the wharf."

And he went ashore with them, one in each hand, his sister just before, and so led the way for the small party up the bank and over to the ancient blockhouse in the field.

Traditions of the old Indian times came in there. Dr. Griffith seemed to know them all; but he appealed courteously to Matthew, and left the narration to him wherever he took it up most confidently. He meant to give the boy his chance in every way.

Afterward, Matthew contrived to be first off to the shore, convoying Miss Rickstack and Jane Gregory.

It was easy to get in advance of Miss Rickstack down there among the shards and fragments of loose rock and the rough projections of the water-worn cliff base. The good lady was busy at once in looking after "queer stones;" besides, she was saying to herself, kind-heartedly, and with a pleasant bit of self-delusion, "We were all young once." Dear, gentle soul! She had been all her life, for her own part, utterly innocent of any sentimental river-side ramblings, or pairings off of any sort. She had not been pretty in her girlhood. As a matter of fact, she had, rather, the parings — if one may be pardoned the unpremeditated play on the word — of all youthful social foregatherings. But there is a point in life, no doubt, where the imaginations of the past take shape into realities through haze of distance, as those of the future used to do. Very likely Miss Rickstack thought she had done such things, or might have done them.

It was out here, among the heaps and débris of time and river work, done through centuries upon rock and soil — as they stood and peered far into a deep crevice that, the story says, runs back into the cliff, away underground, and was once made communicable with the rough stronghold of the early settlers; at least, some such half-hidden fissure did so, and it might well enough be that — that Matt said abruptly, —

" I can't bear to think you are all going off so soon, Miss Gregory. These have been such pleasant days."

"They have been beautiful days," said Jane calmly. " And we have owed much of our enjoyment to you, Mr. Morse."

While she spoke, she moved along to pick up a

clear, soft, gray-white, polished stone, that lay, conspicuous in shape and color, among dark pebbles.

If he had said so much to little Dorothy Serle, the pretty schoolmistress at Beech Point, she would have blushed all up, and caught her breath, and waited, mute and fluttering, for his next word, — a word that he knew in his conscience he had stopped short of many times, in his secret security and his half-readiness to compromise his freedom. He hardly knew what to make of this emotionless Miss Gregory.

"I don't feel satisfied — I wish I need n't think — that all the acquaintance would end here," he said, coming beside her again. "If I should come to Boston, — I might, in the winter, some time, — would you tell me where you would be, and let me call and see you?"

"I do not know exactly where I — where we — shall be, Mr. Morse. I expect to be with Mrs. Sunderland. I dare say·she would be very happy to have you come. But you had better ask her."

Was it shyness, or was it coldness, or was it the sort of encouragement a girl gives when she refers to those who have the guardianship or protection of her?

, He said no more for a few moments, and then made different essay.

"We have never been round Riggsville yet," he said. "It's a pretty row there, up the creek. I'd like to take you one afternoon before you go."

To which assertion, for it stopped short of asking, Jane said "Thank you," without committal; meaning and expecting to be altogether too busy for carrying any such idea into effect.

"Miss Rickstack!" she called, directly after, "there are some lovely things over here. And I do believe I've found an arrowhead."

She stooped and picked up a three-cornered bit of flint, and Miss Rickstack came stumbling across the moraine.

Matthew Morse did not know whether he were rebuffed or not. This kind of courteous, self-possessed reserve was something new to him. It might be a higher tone of coquetry, or a mere decorum; he could not tell. It was not scorn, nor affront. It was too gentle, too tranquil. Whatever it did mean, it meant all the more thoroughly. For the moment he had to be content with that.

But she did not sit at the tiller any more with Matthew, going back. Matthew was interrupted, busy with rope and sail. They had tide in their favor, but the soft wind was ahead. Dr. Griffith managed the rudder for a good while; this left Jane a chance to attach herself to Mrs. Sunderland and the children, which she did with gladness.

Sweeping along with the swift current into the broad bay at sundown, the full glory of that wonderful mingling and play of color in sky and sea and shore broke forth before them. It is impossible to put it into word or picture. The hand of God spreads it out in a few such places; our small, human capacity may merely stand and be filled with it, nor dare to try its reproduction.

Gold and flame-color and pale green in the sky; green and gold repeated in the sea; a far-off amethyst line against the horizon-bend; the lovely hues palpitating, floating, changing, like jewels massed and molten, flowing one into another; shores radiant with answering tints, breathing and shining in rich leafage, mirrored in still margins and clear depths; the creeping inlets all on fire with beauty, whether of the earth, or of the heaven, it were hard to tell; a splendor flung back and forth in echoes of shine and sheen; sleeping, tender shadows waiting their turn to veil all in a yet more exquisite softness, upon which quiet stars will look down with benison, — this is a hint of what lay before their eyes and reached into their spirits, as the sea reaches up into the glowing land.

They all stood forward and watched, Dr. Griffith with them. Margaret drew a long breath and spoke, —

" It must be more beautiful, Hans, than even

what you wrote us of from up that still, sunshiny river. You remember, Jane ? "

She really spoke quite unpremeditatedly. Dr. Griffith turned quickly.

They were all illumined in that universal flush of light; but was it sunset color that mantled Jane's face all over with such revealing brilliancy?

" I remember," spoke up Alice eagerly. " It was the letter that had a seraphim at the end of it."

The laugh was a relief, to one at least. But what followed did not relieve.

" ' A seraphim ' ! What do you mean, dear little child ? " cried Margaret.

" Well, it was something like that. It was the story about the girl that had her hat blow off that uncle Hans told for me; and all about the steamboat, and the river piling up and letting them go by; and the seraphim was something that did n't say much, but meant a good deal. Was n't it, Jane ? "

Jane might blaze, but she stood like her namesake of Arc at the stake. When things were at the worst she had her heroism, — the heroism of a simple directness.

" I remember it very well," she said. " But the word you mean was ' aphorism.' "

She knew it to the last word, then. And all

that about herself which had declared Dr. Griffith's identity to her — and in such fashion — before they met, that second time, in Ascutney Street.

She had known whom to expect to meet. She had known what his first thought of her had been. That was the disclosure now between these two.

A mutual perception was suddenly established between Jane Gregory and Dr. Griffith that could not be ignored, any more than it could, at this instant, be acknowledged or dwelt upon. The flash through one mind was — "How much did that color mean beyond the inevitable embarrassment of appropriating — being known to have appropriated — all that had been said of her in the telling of that little story?" In the other, "He knows, now, how I knew; but he does not seem as if he cared so much as when he first asked me." And Jane held up her head proudly; that a simple fact should appear was neither her fault nor her concern.

John Griffith noted that also. "She lets the truth take care of itself," he thought; and again her brave simplicity laid strong hold of the noblest that was in himself. "She does not look for a sign; she would die rather than have one escape her. She is not a coquette; she is a woman."

At the same instant Margaret scanned the two faces swiftly, and read them both. With lovely tact she reverted to her first question.

"I think this must be even more beautiful than that, John," she said again.

"A second beautiful thing is better understood from having known the first," John answered.

"And that's another aphorism," said Alice quaintly.

Uncle John told her that she ought to patent her system of mnemonics, left her to ask her mother what that meant, and walked away.

Certainly, the knight's move is sometimes very erratic. In the dream of the looking-glass, at every critical juncture, especially of any little triumph or advantage, it was to tumble sidewise off his horse.

"John," said Margaret to Dr. Griffith that night, after the children had gone up to bed with Jane, "the chance is yours. You can't give it to anybody else, if you try. And, John, dear, I'm on your side; and do make haste."

"Gretel! Why what has swept you over, quite to the other extreme?"

"That's the queen's move, isn't it?" asked Margaret, laughing. But the tears were in her eyes. "Don't leave it any longer to that Matthew

Morse," she said softly. "There is n't much time now."

"There is n't any, just at present, Gretel. And I thought you were quite sure. I certainly need not be in haste."

"Sure? Of one thing — yes, I am; but there are so many things."

"I shall be back on Saturday," said Dr. Griffith. And for thanks he took his sister in his arms and kissed her.

"He 'll leave it all. He 'll be off for three days. He thinks it will make no difference. I wonder how men ever *do* get married!" was what Mistress Margaret said, perturbedly, to herself.

"Well, Matt, and how did it go with Ladybird, to-day?" asked old Captain Zenas of his son, as they sat at supper.

"It all went well, father," was the reply.

"And how — with *both* ladybirds, I mean?"

"I think it went well, father. I hope so."

"You 'd be sorry, Matt, if it did n't, would you?"

"I should be more sorry than I know how to be."

He spoke literal truth. He had never learned how to be sorry.

"Somehow — it 's a queer world — somebody

most alwers *hes* to be sorry, whatever happens. Little Dorothy would be sorry, Matt. And may be somebody else would be sorry after that other girl. It's a dreadful queer world. I'm sorry for little Dorothy, myself. I might ha' gone to-day, Matt, I suppose ; but some way, I did n't feel to keer to, quite."

The simple words of his old father found a place in Matthew's heart that had never been reached before.

For the first time in his life he felt what a disappointed hope might be.

Had he given any hope that he might be guilty in disappointing?

Yet how could he help it ? He had never known anything like this before. How could he have understood ?

He got up and went out. He went on board the Ladybird that swung at her quiet mooring. He sat down on the tiller-bench, where Jane had sat.

CHAPTER XV

THOSE next three days were not nice ones for Jane.

" She 's in a wee-waw," said Aunty to Margaret, at last. " And when a woman 's in a wee-waw about *them* things — Lor' sake, Mis' Sunderland, I could n't never 'ave stood it, an' that 's just why I had to leave it alone ! "

Jane was deep in a fixed self-disdain by this time.

What had she treasured up in the memory of that first meeting, like a raw, romance-reading, ignorant girl, to join afterward with the discovery that had been her secret for a while, only to intensify her folly, and that the betrayal of all should come at once, now that it had apparently ceased to be of interest to Dr. Griffith ?

How had she fallen into depreciation with him, slipped from the dignity of simple womanhood, in which he had given her the beginning of a beautiful friendship, to the position of a weak creature toward whom it was a kindness on a man's part to assume cool, guarded distance ?

Margaret was even sweeter than ever. Was this a woman's compassion for a woman in such strait, — sunken to such evident, pitiable self-abandonment that all must do what could be done to silently help her up from it?

The temptation did come upon her, transiently, to give utter contradiction to this need in the most positive way; a way that, had it not been shut to her by this very foolishness, she could even see might have been a good way.

How did she know but this was what was truly meant for her, and that she should grow content, once having put the other irrevocably out of her thought?

She should have God and his beautiful world, anyway; if He put her here, in this Paradise of his, should she not thank Him and serve Him, — " acquaint herself with Him, and be at peace " ?

Did Eve look about in Eden, or out into the wilderness, for any other than the Adam by whose side — because, without her choice, she was of his side — the Lord had set her?

Ah, but this being of a man — one living flesh with him in God's own sight — what strange bewilderment had Eden come to, in this crowded world where each — brought into casual personal presence with but few, and so imperfectly — must find and choose out of the millions of a generation her very own?

One's own could not come to every one. Should she take another's then?

No; she could stay alone. Because a little door — too low and narrow for her, like the one in Alice's dream — was the only one she could discover, must she drink that strange and perilous draught which would make her spiritually small enough to enter?

She thought these things all out within herself while busy, outwardly, with the children and the trunks and the packing; while she told stories and played games with them on that rainy Thursday and dull Friday that followed their enchanted summer sail.

She stayed upstairs when Matthew Morse came in below; he did not like to ask for her, and so escape was easy. She thought she could keep on escaping for just these few days; if not, whatever she had to do would not be her fault.

She was only determined that it should not be that row to Riggsville.

The Saturday came, clear but cooler. The wind was from the west, with now and then a snap of north in it. Matthew Morse came round in the morning with his yacht; he was going to Squirrel Island to take a party up to Bath on their way home. The children ran in to tell that he had left his rowboat — that pretty Dragonfly — in the little cove.

" Be sure you don't go near it," said Mrs. Sunderland. "You promise ? "

Rick and Alice promised their mother aloud; Jane promised herself as positively in silence.

In the afternoon they were all out in the warm pine grove behind the cottage ; it was still and sheltered there ; it had been their favorite resort in the latter part of the day, with their books and work. They sat there now, rather more wrapped in shawls and sacques than made work convenient; but covetous of every last hour in every pleasant place.

The children were feeding some squirrels that had grown tame enough to come almost within their reach for crumbs. They were watching them scud along a regular route, from the big old tree where they had their nest in a hollow, — up its shaggy trunk, out on its farthest-reaching knobby branch; a flight across to the tip of the low, horizontal stretch of the next one ; up and down and across from limb to limb, one little plumy-tailed fellow after another, with always the same turns and runs and springs, which the children were never tired of following, — till they stood with their bright eyes glancing this way and that, tails waving and arching, chattering, scolding ; the same invariable hesitation at the same point about coming nearer, which was always overcome at last in the same way, till down they rushed — "a whole stream of squirrels," Alice said — over the back of the last bent stem to where she and Rick had strewed bits of bread and apple, to fill their cheeks with these, and then scamper off over their "branch-road," to a safe perch where they could take "three minutes for refreshments," and munch in comfort.

"We shall miss them so !" said the little people.

"But we shall have Daisy and Dandelion, and Shag and Shock, and all the new kittens at Bay Hill," said their mother. "And may be next year we will come and see the squirrels again."

She could not help glancing at Jane as she said that ; and that Jane's face was of an unreadable stillness only offered a blank into which Mrs. Sunderland thought she could put for herself some easy syllables.

The tip of a white sail, like a bird's wing, appeared above the green edge of the bank beyond them, where the hill sloped steeply to the narrow channel on the Southport side. It slid along, seeming to cleave a way between the soft, blending lines of either shore.

"It is Matt come back!" cried Rick. "May n't we go down now, mamma?"

Jane let go her self - command, and half lost her head.

Startling from the thought of what might next be expected of her with the children, she sprang to her feet and spoke hurriedly, confusedly, to Mrs. Sunderland.

"Would you please — excuse me — just a little while? I can't — I want to go — I have a headache — I 'd like a walk, all by myself," she said.

She tied the strings of her gypsy hat firmly under her chin, for the wind was brisk; it made a soft, continual rush overhead there, in the tops of the thick pines.

"Take your shawl," said Mrs. Sunderland, assenting as of course.

Now the shawl was a soft, knit thing, of cardinal red.

"Oh, no!" Jane answered, with quick positiveness. "My jacket will do." And she buttoned it closer, as she turned and sped swiftly off between the dark trees.

It was then that Aunty said to Margaret that the girl was in a wee-waw.

Jane kept in the grove as far as it reached; then she hastened across toward the ridge, through a little dip in the pasture land beyond; choosing a harder path and farther from the cove than the one she had climbed with Dr. Griffith, that she might make the shelter of a group of cedars, and reach the top beyond it, where she would not be observed from anywhere about the cottage.

She had the fleeing instinct upon her, which seizes a creature bodily when the mind finds no safe way to turn ; to get off as far as she could — to be alone — to escape everything, became a wild desire.

In the mean time, Matthew came up through the orchard into the pines, met Mrs. Sunderland, and asked with direct purpose for Miss Gregory.

"She has a headache," said that lady. "She has gone off to be quiet. I am sorry, — but — I do not think she would wish to be sent for."

Matt's face fell.

"I came to ask her to have a row with me — over to Riggsville."

"I'm afraid it's out of the question; and, isn't it rather too windy for comfort, anyway ?" asked Mrs. Sunderland, willing to soften with external reason the personal refusal.

"You feel it more on shore than you need to on the water," answered Matt. "Among these islands you can always get under the lee of something. That's the beauty of being landlocked. You can row or sail, when you couldn't walk upon the cliffs. It may blow for an hour or two, but it 'll calm down by sunset. Don't you think it might do her good, perhaps, to go?"

His eyes met Mrs. Sunderland's as he spoke, and if ever a man's eyes said anything to a woman's, there were words in his at that moment. "Ah, do be on my side!" they plainly besought.

Margaret's heart smote her that it had come to this. She must be on his side; but it could not be as he asked. It must be to spare him; she had to look steadily, kindly, at him, and reply, "I do not think so."

Then Matthew broke forth, "How much don't you think, Mrs. Sunderland? I want to see her. I shall have so little chance now. I know it is too soon — for her; but it 's all dead sure with me. I want to ask her — just to remember me," said the poor fellow; and drops stood with the flush upon his forehead.

Margaret knew what real mercy was.

"Matthew," she said, "we all like you too well to be willing to hurt you. And so *I think* there is something you will have to give up."

"You think; but you do not know?"

"I will find out for you, Matthew; I believe I have found out already; I wish I could have seen sooner, for I might have saved you something. But I will be honest for you now, and I will tell you honestly."

And with that Matthew Morse had to go away.

An hour and a half later, the little steamer touched at Leeport Landing, and Dr. Griffith came ashore.

He found Margaret in the cottage parlor, pale, uneasy. "O John!" she cried, "she has been gone, alone, this ever so long, and the wind blows so! She must have gone a strange, long way."

"What did she go for?"

"Because Matt Morse came for her, with his boat."

"You mean she went with him?"

"Oh, no, no! she would n't. She went off out of his way."

"Did she go up the ridge?" John Griffith asked; and Margaret guessed from his tone and look the danger.

"Oh, I don't know! She was just wild to get off; she may have gone anywhere!"

John took two tall sticks from the parlor corner: one was his own alpenstock, iron-pointed; the other a stout oak pole, trimmed and ferruled.

He went to the door and whistled. Sachem, a splendid spaniel, — until lately with his brother, Sagamore, the property of the old farmer, Azel Morse, but in these recent weeks, by that instinctive friendship which attaches chosen beast to chosen man, and by exchange of value in dollars,

transferred to Dr. Griffith — Sachem, who had
just met his master at the landing and tumultu-
ously escorted him homeward, came rushing in delightedly.

"Give me something of hers — ah, this will do,"
and the doctor picked up the little red shawl which
he knew quite well. He held it for the dog to
sniff, then rolled it up under his arm.

"Where did she start from?" he asked Margaret.

"From the bench under the two pines," she told
him. "But oh, Hans! are you going on the cliff?
How shall I know — how can you tell — what may
have happened, — whether you can do, alone?"

"Give me your handkerchief," he said. "I
will send Sachem back with this; if I tie a knot in
it, all is well, and I want nothing; if he brings it
loose, send help. Now you may be easy."

There had not been two minutes lost; the doctor
was off, first to the little bench between the trees,
where he gave Sachem the scent again.

"Follow! Find!" he commanded; and the
dog, after circling and sniffing a moment, darted
away over the soft brown needle-mould, in the way
Jane had taken.

Jane, meanwhile, had at first pushed on mechanically, without thought or calculation as to distance
or return.

She had gained the crest of the ridge, and upon its broader, northern stretch, like a high moor, had walked on, with plenty of leeway for yielding to the force of the keen, bright wind, which rather nerved and toned her for exertion than gave her any anxiety. She leaned against it, as it were, and let it help her forward, as with a kind, strong hand. There was a certain comfort in feeling its support and urging; she had so little else to lean against, in any sense, just now!

It came in sweeps and lulls. If she had been more weatherwise, this gusty character would have warned her of the more possible risk; as it was, she kept on, the inward impulse still driving her forward, and a secret desire drawing her toward the wild, beautiful spot where she had spent one such marvelous hour. Above everything, as she had said; to get above, beyond, — this was her prompting now, simply to escape; by and by she must do her own thinking, her resolving. The future must be all redetermined, perhaps; but she would not look at it yet.

On; over the scrambling, difficult gaps and outcrops; up and down the cross ridges, like great vertebræ of a colossal spine, to the beginning of the narrow neck with the steep, inward incline on one side, and the jagged, seaward precipices on the other.

It did not take long to cross; in those moments the wind madé one of its brief pauses. Jane climbed and clung well; she was safely over to the head of the cliff-fissure which she had descended with Dr. Griffith.

Once below the frowning top, she was in a calm; no touch of the wind reached her. She did not venture quite so far as the doctor had led her, but found a scooped-out hollow, part way down, with a bolstering edge of rough rock forward; here she placed herself, and set her spirit free into that wide, glorious distance.

It was as if all troubling, impassioned thoughts that had been bound in upon herself, chafing and fretting like caged things, were let loose upon the living air that lifted them from her and bore them away, lost in its overflowing vastness.

She sat there, breathing quietness, expanding into strength.

Above her, the wind rose in higher, more impetuous gusts. It smote itself against the rough inland steep, and swirled upward. It rushed, viewless, from the lip of the crag over her head. Across the jagged bridge that she had passed, it swept clean, resistless. She could not have stood there now.

Half an hour later, she clambered upward, and met it in its face.

Happily, the fissure path led round a point of crag that was between her and the sea. Against this she paused, almost pinned there by the gale.

She crept and struggled a little way, on hands and knees, then wedged herself into a side crevice, and waited.

How should she ever cross that *mauvais pas* ?

It stretched before her ; she could see its length ; it was like the neck of a great animal whose head was turned toward the sea. Just in the turn, below the beetling uplift of the head itself, was her own safe, small nestling-place. But how long could she stay there ? How long before the wind would all rush by ?

" It goes down with the sun," she had heard the country people say, in such a fair-weather blow. If it would only calm so that she might crawl over!

She studied out a possible pathway in the cracks and windings that she could see, from rock to rock. If there came any cessation she must try, she must begin.

At the outset of a pain or a peril, it never seems that it can last. It had not been blowing like that a half hour before. Why should it blow on a half hour longer ? But every minute that she waited there seemed ten.

For a good while she did not give way to abso- lute terror. But it came at last. She trembled all over as she sat there. What if it should last all night?

She bent her head down upon her knees, and prayed to Him who ruleth the storm.

She never knew how long it had been, when she caught a distant sound borne toward her by the very blast — the sharp, quick bark of a dog; the voice of a man who cheered him on. They were coming for her.

Who was coming? And how had anybody known?

She stood up and watched along that rugged side-slant. Between the wall of wind and the wall of cliff she was held, with only a half yard's width for her feet.

Upon the broader, humping shoulder of the huge ledge-form, she saw, presently, the man. A tall, strong figure that advanced just under the crest, the wind holding him, as it did her, away from the descent. He could not come much further, so.

She cried out to him to stop; but the wind whirled her voice off into the great spaces with its own. She stretched out her arms, her hands held up, palms forward, bidding him back with the gesture. Then she sat down, quietly, to show him she was safe and self-possessed.

The dog stood and bayed at her, half in triumph

half at fault. She could only guess what his master said to him, and interpret it by the dog's action.

"Down, Sachem! Charge!" and the docile,
sagacious creature crouched and planted himself
at Dr. Griffith's feet, his nose level toward Jane,
his bright eye fixed on her, she knew, as in his
keeping.

Dr. Griffith leaned back against the shelving
bank, and took his memorandum book from his
pocket. He wrote a few lines upon a bit of paper,
and tucked this tightly into the little red shawl
bundle which he had tied round with a bit of
string. The ends of the string he fastened to the
dog's collar, and put the soft roll into Sachem's
mouth. "Now, give it to her!" he shouted, and
pointed over at Jane.

Where two feet and greater height could not
have gone — through gullies and crannies, choosing
the safest track, sometimes scrambling along under
the overhanging edge upon the island side, his tail
held gallantly aloft, with silken fringes that the
wind blew like a cavalier's plume — came Sachem,
struggling, proud, hilarious, and laid his muzzle,
presently, with the burden in charge, upon Jane's
knees.

On the slip of paper was written, — again it was
a recipe blank that he had taken, — "Keep as you

are until I come to you. Make Sachem stay. I will wait and watch my chance ; the wind will lull. Do not be afraid."

Jane laid her hand on the dog's head. " Charge, Sachem ! " she said softly. And Sachem, obeying the gentle breath as if it had been the sternest order, laid himself down beside her, his chin across her feet.

Jane wrapped the red shawl around her, crossed it over her breast, and tied it fast behind.

On each side the intervening danger, they waited. They bided their time in each other's sight, each still and patient that the other might be likewise.

In this parable of circumstance, thoughts — perhaps they were hardly definite — moved between them that they might never speak. They were separated ; but the very separation drew them close.

Jane felt in a strange peace. He was there ; he would come to her. He would not be in any reckless haste. He would do the right thing. When it was time, he would be by her side.

John Griffith waited but to claim his own. He knew now that it was his own ; that it should be, through whatever stress, whatever forces of interruption.

On either side a deeper abyss, with fiercer blast — even the rushing, invisible mights that part the worlds — between them, they would yet stay but for the moment that should bring them hand to hand again, ay, soul to soul.

Had they not found each other in all the wonderful stretch and surge of time and mystery of causes, — the seeming random of birth and place and incident, — and how should anything fail them now?

CHAPTER XVI.

THE muteness and the pause were deep and grand with meanings that no easy lover's talk could ever touch. The power about them that held them so — that with its own great voice hushed theirs — was not a dread or threat; it was assurance, promise.

The gale began to catch its breath. As the sun went lower, and the air cooled over the sea, it came less impetuously down into the ocean spaces from its mountain heights; it rested; it panted; then for an instant it would sweep on again. But its velocity was less terrible; down in the low places it would be but a lively breeze.

At the first real check, Dr. Griffith moved. He had made cool calculation; he had mapped his track, partly following Sachem's instinctive lead. He knew where he could plant his alpenstock, in those rough slants and crevices, and keep his feet this side the perilous crest-edge. He had strapped his soft felt hat tightly to his head; he would have no absurdities of inconvenience here. He could stoop, or creep, if need be; he would set his strong limbs and stalwart frame compact against the danger; he would grasp the very hillside and get over there to Jane.

And so he did get over. And down beside the dog he sat himself, on what length was left of the rock-shelf; his feet and alpenstock holding him against a break of the ledge below.

"Jane!" He said the little name boldly, and looked up at her face with something of fun in his eyes, now that he had found her and they were both safe. For he was sure, now, that he could help her across; now, he could do almost anything.

"Jane!" He said it twice. She looked at him, and a brightness broke all over her face.

" Dr. — Hansell! " she answered, with a timid ripple in her voice.

"A high wind seems to be an essential element in our history."

" It is growing calmer now."

" Yes; every moment. It will be beautiful soon. Come, will you trust yourself with me ? "

He got up as he spoke, braced with one knee against the rock; he put the strong oak staff into her right hand; changed his alpenstock into his left; reached up to her with his right arm, and lifted her along beside him.

" Go, Sachem ! " he ordered. " Back, sir ! "

He could not point his command; neither hand

was free. But Sachem knew well enough; the bright fellow set his plume on high, and was off. And they two followed.

Carefully, holding her close to himself on the one side as he bore against the still vigorous wind on the other, bidding her where to step and where to set her stick, he conquered the difficult way with her and for her, point by point.

He only spoke the few words of guidance that she needed, until he had her beyond the pass; then he seated her for a moment, took a handkerchief from his breast-pocket, tied it in a knot, and called Sachem.

The dog, careering back and forth upon the broader height, came close. His master put the handkerchief between his teeth. "Go home!" he said. "Carry!" Sachem looked wistfully an instant, then turned and sped.

"That is to let Margaret know that you are safe," he told her.

He had called her Jane; speaking to herself, he called his sister Margaret. There was some quite new assumption, some strong, gentle claim, in word and tone.

"I shall take you by another path, a downward climb; we will go home by the shore, where it is still. A little further we shall find the way."

He held her fast again as they crossed obliquely

to the seaward brow, and lifted her there into the entrance of a long gully, whose rough depth gave them shelter as they followed it down the broken scrag toward the narrow strip of beach where the hungry sea was lapping.

Alternately leading and lifting her, or giving her hands a strong grasp for a spring across from rock to rock, he piloted her safely till they stood upon the rim of sand, behind which the whole towering ridge stood guard between them and the defeated northwest wind.

The warmth of the sunny day was sleeping here still; they had but to walk in the sweet stillness upon which the low whisper of the slow-curling comb was the only break, till they came to the spur of rock around or over which they would reach the sandy cove.

Dr. Griffith did not mean to be in any haste. He made Jane sit down at the foot of the cliff, and stood beside her while she rested.

"Jane," he said again, "why did you do all this?" He asked as if he meant to know.

And Jane knew he never put a question lightly. She looked at him with clear eyes, and answered with gentle bravery, —

" I wanted to get away."

" From what, please ? "

" I think — from myself, as much as anything."

" And did you ? "

" Yes. Myself was scattered into spray and carried off out of me, over that great sea."

John Griffith looked down into her face until her face looked down again from him.

" Well, I forgive you, since it has given us this, together," he said. " This is nearly our last day with the sea, you know."

" I know."

" It is hard to give the New England grandeur up, and go off to bury one's self in the heart of the continent."

" Except that there is, I suppose, a motive, — a work to do that could not be done here," said Jane. " There are such strong motives for men — in a world that wants men all over it ! "

" Can you think of any motive that would take a woman there, — a woman who loved the sea and hills as — you do ? "

Hesitation was committal. If this were an ordinary question, the answer must be instant.

A color crept up over Jane's throat and cheek and brow ; she dared not even turn her head aside, that the gypsy hat might screen it. She kept her eyes quiet and steadfast, looking out upon the level water.

"I can think there might be motives that would take a woman anywhere," she said, strong and low.

"I can think of but one woman that I would ask to go. Could you — will you — go to Sunnywater with me? Will you belong to me, Jane?"

Jane sat still; utterly silent. The greatness of that which had come to her hushed her — held her motionless.

"Am I asking too much?" said Dr. Griffith.

Then she rose up and stood before him, as Ruth might have stood before Boaz.

"You are giving me more than I could think God ever meant for me," she told him.

. . . .

They reached the cottage in the dim twilight, and Margaret met them at the porch.

"She is your sister, Margaret," said John; and Margaret took her in her arms, and held her close, and kissed her.

. . . .

The next morning was full of peace and sun. shine. The Sunday blessedness was in and over everything.

"I am going to take you to the undercliff again, Jane," Dr. Griffith said, after the breakfast was finished, and they were out in the fresh air before the door. "I want a clear, sure daylight talk with you, — and I want it there."

The last sentence was for her ear only.

The children caught the word of the walk. "May we go too?" cried Alice.

Margaret took the little girl's hand. "Not this time, Alice. Uncle Hans wants your White Queen all to himself."

The child looked wonderingly from one to another, weighing the meaning of the answer. Her mother never made her an evasive one.

Something — who shall say what — touched the hidden woman-heart in her, and gave her a vague, sweet apprehension. She came and stood close before the two.

"Uncle Hans," she said, "I'll lend you my White Queen. Queen, I'll lend you uncle Hans. But you must be very particular of each other, for I'm very particular of you both!"

The little rowboat came round into the cove, while Jane and Dr. Griffith were far out toward the lighthouse point.

Matt had come to see Mrs. Sunderland, and he found her with her book in a sunny corner of the rocks.

"Do you know what I want to know?" he asked her. "Have you come to tell me?"

"Yes, Matthew. We shall all be your friends, always. But you will have to give it up."

The young fellow crushed his hat as he held it between his knees, and said never a word.

"It has only been a few weeks," said Margaret kindly. "All your life is behind it, and all that is to be your life is before. You must not let this one point be all to you, or spoil it all."

"It might have made it all!" exclaimed Matthew bitterly. "And now — it may never be made. May I not say anything to her?"

"It will make you more sorry if you do," said Margaret. "I am dealing truly with you, for I know." He felt that there was something behind her words.

"You have been kind to me, at any rate," he said to her.

"Yes, we have both tried to be kind — my brother and I. Whatever happens, believe that."

"What *will* happen?" he demanded quickly, grasping the truth that she would fain not have given him all at once. "Where is she now?"

Mrs. Sunderland laid her hand on his. "They are away — walking — to the lighthouse rocks," she said.

He sat still for several moments; he held himself so, for pride's sake and for the sake of that sweet, womanly touch, slowly withdrawn. Then he got up, and she stood also.

The little boat, lying dragged up on the sand, lifted her pretty, painted bow toward them. The Dragonfly. The name and the winged creature named for were on the prow, in brilliant, delicate color-drawing.

" You find such pretty things to call your vessels by," said Mrs. Sunderland, in the way one does say a pleasant irrelevant word, to escape a relevant one, or a hard silence.

Matthew Morse shot a glance at her, which she answered as she interpreted it.

" Don't think I don't care, Matt; you have a way of finding right things; you will find right things in your life."

A moment more and he had gone, with her words like arrows in his heart.

" Right things."

And Dorothy Serle had found the pretty names for him. And Dorothy Serle had painted the slender, gauze-winged dragonfly for him, that no coarse, common workman could have done.

.   .   .   .

Jane went back to Ascutney Street. She fulfilled her ten days with Mrs. Turnbull. When she had sewed the last tape loop inside the waistband of the last completed garment, and had hung it in the spare-chamber closet where Mrs. Turnbull kept the " poor sheep and silkworm " part of her as in a shrine, she said to that lady that she had finished.

" Well, — what now ? " was the rejoinder. Mrs. Turnbull had decided that she would keep Jane, on the old terms, manage it as she might ; but she left it to Jane herself to say some word to lead to it.

Jane's answer took her by surprise, now that the Sunderlands had gone home — " to the country," Jane had said. There was no other place, she thought, for the girl; and she credited herself with magnanimity in holding her own door open — after all.

" I am going to Bay Hill," Jane said.

" Where's Bay Hill? "

" Out beyond Exham."

" Who lives there? Who do you work for? "

" Myself, I think, this time. Mrs. Sunderland lives there. Mrs. Turnbull, I am going to be married."

" *Married !* " It was not a question. Jane replied nothing to the mere explosion.

" *You !* " The second exclamation had the astonishment of the impossible in it, as if Jane must be making plans all by herself in life, which ordinarily took two to accomplish.

" I — and another person," Jane explained accordingly, with a smile.

" Of course. Who is it? "

" John Griffith. He is Mrs. Sunderland's brother."

" H—m ! H'm ! H——m ! *That's* it ! I dare say you 'll do very well, Jane ; very suitably. · I hope so, I'm sure. But you've been very quiet. Where did you ever see John Griffith?"

"At Leeport. And before that, two years ago."

"All that time! Well,—it's unriddled now," said Mrs. Turnbull sharp-pointedly.

Jane did not open matters further by asking what was unriddled. She thought she had been explanatory enough.

.   .   .   .

Mrs. Turnbull told the news to her husband, with her usual involutions.

"I suppose she thinks she's bettering herself. They all do," was her preliminary.

"It's a human delusion," said Mr. Turnbull.

"And it's been going on these two years, and she never said a word!"

"Waiting for the last word, I suppose, so that she could put it in good shape first," responded the gentleman. "It wouldn't do to begin at the beginning."

"I wish you'd listen! It's Jane Gregory; she won't come here any more; she's going to Bay Hill, wherever that is, with Mrs. Sunderland; she's going to be married to Mrs. Sunderland's brother, a man by the name of John Griffith; there!"

"Wh—e—ew!"

"Whatever are you whistling at? It isn't anything *very* extraordinary, after all."

" Griffith! Sunderland! Bay Hill!" ejaculated Mr. Turnbull. " Old lady, you 've just missed the best chance you ever had in all your life; and Rebecca Louisa Rickstack's got it!"

Now Mrs. Turnbull had never been near Rebecca Rickstack since the latter came home from Leeport.

" Do you know — Jane Gregory's going right — slap — in — amongst the very first chop — A 1, registered at Lloyd's?" demanded Mr. Turnbull, who liked to be mercantile, but who mixed his phrases.

" No! How?" gasped Mrs. Turnbull, reduced to simplicity and directness.

" Griffith and Sunderland. Old L—— Wharf. Griffith of Wall Street. Boston *and* New York. Rich as thunder. Biggest swells going. What in time brought any of 'em to Ascutney Street?"

" I don't believe the girl knows it herself. I don't believe it 's them," panted Mrs. Turnbull, losing both breath and grammar.

" True as revelation. She 's got the dead wood on you, Lorry-Laviny!" And he left Lorry-Laviny to recover, and went off to bed.

.   .   .   .

Jane stayed till early spring at Bay Hill. When it came to the trousseau, Mrs. Sunderland said that was to be her part. Jane put her arm round her, and thanked her with kisses, but declared there was no need. "I have nearly six hundred dollars for it," she told her; "and I'm so glad!"

But more than six hundred other dollars were dropped in, in casual contributions, besides the stated, stately bridal gift in orthodox silver.

Miss Rickstack came to the wedding. The Turnbulls were invited. Do you think they went?

Mrs. Turnbull did; her husband could not leave his business in the morning.

"Of course; why shouldn't I?" the Ascutney Street lady said. "I was her first friend. I picked her up when she was nowhere. If it hadn't been for me, she wouldn't have been anywhere now. I shall send her a butterknife."

So she did; and a week after the wedding-day, she went out to Bay Hill again, and called on Mrs. Sunderland.

Mrs. Turnbull really thought Ascutney Street did it; and that henceforth Ascutney Street might claim relationship with Bay Hill. Through Miss Rickstack it did; she was never "set down" again, or forgotten. And through Miss Rickstack and The Crocus crept an inner influence that made a link of reality.

The good ladies were gradually less afraid of the honest truths of their existence; less eagerly

anxious about the visible aspects. "Miss Rickstack did thus and so;" and Miss Rickstack stayed
at Bay Hill days and days together, and had the
Sunderlands to take tea or stay to lunch, without
ever making either "teas" or "lunches."

They began to find out that a mere shell of cus-
tom, precisely like that convenient to their own
living, was not the thing these truly fine people
always looked for, by which to fasten their best
associations with the lives of others.

Mrs. Sunderland had caught the right one in her
little "trap" of genuineness, and had let her go to
good result among her comrades. Miss Rickstack
ruled Ascutney Street, and was uplifting it; but
there was never a meeker, more unconscious poten-
tate.

Mrs. Turnbull thought things were growing very
common there. It was a failure for her, and in a
year or two she moved away.

Mrs. Sunderland had received her wedding-party
call politely, but had never initiated further civilities.

.   .   .   .

I had to come back to Ascutney Street at the
end, for we began there, and it is there the little
moral of my story lies, if it has one; but I should
like to take you all the way out to Sunnywater.

I should like to show you the long, low house
from which the beautiful turf spreads away in

slopes and swells under the great black-walnuts; I should like to show you the rooms inside, lovely with every touch and sign of heart-abidingness, but not " decorated " with anything.

I should like to have you see Dr. Griffith come riding home at night on his fine bay that he calls Sagamore, for Sachem's brother, with Sachem bounding at his heels; see the doctor fling the bridle on the horse's neck, while. Bat Knutsen takes him by the bit to lead him to his stable; while John Griffith puts his arm round Jane, waiting for him at the door, and they go off together to watch the sunset at a certain point where it blazes across a distant, wonderful vista; while Mrs. Knutsen gets the tea upon the table — " the yems and the yonny-cake and the yinyer," with a steak or a prairie chicken for substantial — to have all ready when the two shall come in again, happy with hunger, and hungry with happiness.

" Is it as good as it may have been among the islands, two hours ago? " asks Dr. Griffith, standing with his wife in the glory that sweeps from a far horizon line, over one knows not what between, into this noble woodland colonnade, to drop at their feet its long-sped, splendid shafts. " Is it as good for you as that, or must we go to Sheepscote River? "

And Jane says, in that peculiar way of hers, as

if thought felt itself carefully into the truest words, —

" Everything is as good as everything. The day is n't over till it has all got lighted up; the world is round, and life is as round as the world, John!"

THE END.